"COME WITH US." The guards grabbed Alex and ushered him away.

They finally stopped in front of a pair of ornate doors, the kind Alex had seen only in movies. One of the guards knocked on the doors, then pushed them open. Alex saw a large room, brightly decorated with floor-to-ceiling murals of sea creatures and bull dancers, pictures of parties and festivals, but also scenes of war and destruction.

The guards led Alex to the center of the room and left him there.

"Wait here and don't move," their leader ordered. "We'll be right outside."

They closed the door behind them as they left. Alex was alone. . . .

MythQuest

BOOK I

The Minotaur

A novelization by
Tom Mason and Dan Danko
Based on the teleplay by Morrie Ruvinsky

BANTAM BOOKS
New York · Toronto · London · Sydney · Auckland

RL 5.5, AGES 10 and up

THE MINOTAUR

A Bantam Skylark Book / January 2003

ISBN: 0-553-48759-0 (pbk.)
0-553-13009-9 (lib. bdg.)

**Visit us on the Web! www.randomhouse.com/kids
Educators and librarians, for a variety of teaching tools,
visit us at www.randomhouse.com/teachers**

Published simultaneously in the United States and Canada
Bantam Skylark is an imprint of Random House Children's
Books, a division of Random House, Inc. SKYLARK BOOK
and colophon and BANTAM BOOKS and colophon are
registered trademarks of Random House, Inc. Bantam Books,
1540 Broadway, New York, New York 10036.

PRINTED IN THE UNITED STATES OF AMERICA

OPM 10 9 8 7 6 5 4 3 2 1

MythQuest

Book I

The Minotaur

Prologue

Acheon stumbled blindly down the narrow passage. The only sound he could hear was his heart pounding violently against his chest like a deafening drum overwhelming a chorus of gentle violins. His throat was sore, and each rapid breath stung more sharply than the last.

The passage was dimly lit. Torches protruded from the walls. The licking flames cast shadows that fluttered on the ground like dancing ghosts. He gripped the base of a torch and tried desperately to pull it from the wall. It wasn't much, but at least it would be a weapon. His nails dug into the wood; his hands turned beet red as he mustered every ounce of strength to break the torch from its sconce—with no success.

He fell back in defeat. His eyes darted from left to right, searching for a way out. The wall was more than twelve feet high. An equally bleak ceiling choked off the sky. A fine sand spread under his feet, and the gray walls of the passageway stretched forty feet before and behind.

Acheon ran. He ran to the end of the passage, which ended in a T. Without much thought, he bolted to the left and ran for several seconds before he found himself at a four-way intersection. He spun around. His mind raced, and blood pumped so quickly through his veins that its urgency matched his own growing panic. He moved left—no, right. It was right, he was sure. He stumbled forward.

How long had Acheon been running down this maze of corridors? Five minutes? Hours? Days? It had been long enough for his legs to scream in pain with each step, long enough for his stomach to twist with worry—or was that just the fear that continued to drown his senses and told him, *"Run! Run! Run!"*

He raced down another passageway, followed by a second, then a third. Had he been this way before? Was he going in circles? The grayness leaped out at him with a startling sameness. Finally, he stopped for a moment and tried to calm down. This would never work: the running, the panic. He needed a plan.

Acheon collected his thoughts. Yes, a plan. That would certainly be a step in the right direction. It would be difficult, but not impossible. He knelt in the sand to catch his breath. He was strong, a good fighter. Once, he had even bested four foes single-handed. Where was that confidence now? He touched the star-shaped amulet that had been given to him by his parents, a lone green jewel set in its center. As a feeling of reassurance warmed his limbs, a shadow fell over Acheon. He spun.

The creature was large, much larger than he had been told. It had a stink that attacked his nostrils like bees defending their hive. The creature's piercing screech burst from its maw as it fell upon Acheon, its red eyes burning with maddening fury.

The star amulet fell from Acheon's hands. He never had a chance to scream.

Chapter One

Dr. Matt Bellows wiped a smudge from his glasses and checked the clock: 3 A.M. So soon? He checked the coffee cup. Empty. Already?

"Hey, beautiful," Dr. Bellows quipped, unpacking a large sculpture from a wooden crate. Even in the dim light of the desk lamp, the green surface of the statue called the Ch'ang-o seemed to pulse with an inexplicable radiance.

"Open CyberMuseum. Prepare for scan," he said into the computer's microphone. He used both hands to place the heavy Ch'ang-o on the scanner bed. "Begin scan."

The plasma screen before Dr. Bellows blinked to life. The warm green scanner lights danced on the Ch'ang-o, recording every etched nuance, and an exact 3D duplicate of the Ch'ang-o appeared in the center of the plasma screen, floating in midair like an angel's feather.

Dr. Bellows was the most respected archaeologist in the field of computer analysis of artifacts and ruins of ancient civilizations, and the CyberMuseum was the culmination of decades of his research. Spending a few late nights scanning objects was the easy part, compared to the years of study and labor.

The sculpture was simple yet elegant, an odd juxtaposition, with Ch'ang-o, the beautiful Chinese moon goddess, riding atop her demon frog, its legs outstretched as if in midleap. Whether she was the pursuer or the one being pursued was a mystery the priceless carving challenged all onlookers to answer for themselves.

The computer's modem rang. Dr. Bellows tapped the light mouse and a pop-up window appeared in the corner.

"You took it home! Are you crazy?" Barbara Frazier yelled from the computer screen the instant her image appeared.

"Who is this?" Dr. Bellows replied, squinting at the screen.

"Don't mess around, Matt," Barbara hissed back. "You had no right to take the Ch'ang-o."

Something on the screen caught Dr. Bellows's eye, and it wasn't Barbara's scowling face. The 3D rendering of the Ch'ang-o still rotated on the screen. In the middle of the frog was a nearly invisible shape.

"Odd," Dr. Bellows whispered, then, "Hello? Barb? Can you hear me?"

"Don't do this to me!" Barbara yelled back.

"Hello? Hello? I'm losing you!" Dr. Bellows urgently replied, then intentionally disconnected Barbara.

Her image blipped from the screen.

"Set: Contrast level four. Ultraviolet scan," he said.

Screen colors shifted. Light gradations of hue became sharp contrasts of color. The shape in the Ch'ang-o's belly sharpened. Dr. Bellows was certain of one undeniable fact: It was no flaw.

It was a rock buried in the belly of the frog like a swallowed nugget of gold. He recognized it the moment he saw the spearhead and shaft piercing the rock's surface.

Dr. Bellows leaped from his desk. He fumbled through several books. But how could he find an image of something that wasn't supposed to exist? How could he find a photo of something that wasn't supposed to be real?

Dr. Bellows reached out with his finger to the image on the screen, almost afraid to touch it.

"I've found the Gorgos Stone."

He gently pushed the left eye of the real Ch'ang-o, figuring there was a release mechanism somewhere. Nothing. He pulled the goddess's arm while turning the frog's head.

The statue separated into several pieces like a child's puzzle. In the heart of the chunks rested the Gorgos Stone.

Dr. Bellows eagerly inspected it: skull-like, with a single crystal arrow piercing its center. The arrow shaft was riddled with mysterious glyphs. The Gorgos Stone stood on the list of myths alongside Atlantis, the Fountain of Youth, and the Holy Grail.

"Computer: Store Ch'ang-o, Chinese Room Five." Dr. Bellows placed the stone on the scanner.

The computer obeyed. A light glowed beneath the Gorgos Stone, and Dr. Bellows watched with unbelieving eyes as the stone transferred to the screen and completely disappeared from the scanner bed.

"Impossible!" Dr. Bellows gasped. He tried to stop the process, but it was too late. The Gorgos Stone now existed only on the plasma screen.

"What have I done?" he cried.

Chapter Two

Alex Bellows stared out the window. It was a beautiful day, perfect for everything except sitting in class and listening to a lecture, but that was exactly what Alex was doing—except for the listening part. Alex was a good student when he wanted to be, but right now was not one of those times.

The teacher, Juan Watt, turned from the blackboard and immediately noticed Alex's daydreaming.

"Bellows? Do you know the answer?" he asked. Despite the fact that Mr. Watt ran a tight ship, the teacher was actually popular with the students.

Alex snapped to attention. "The answer?" he repeated, hoping to buy time. Historical dates, names, and places flashed through his head. It was only a matter of guessing the right one—like winning a lottery.

"Abraham Lincoln?" Alex asked tentatively, hoping to narrow the odds with a popular historical answer.

"I'm sure Lincoln is the answer to many questions in this class," Mr. Watt replied. "But no, he was not the first man on the moon."

The class laughed. Even Alex cracked a smile as his cheeks grew bright red with embarrassment.

Alex thought that Mr. Watt occasionally singled him out to make an example of him. If Alex's dad hadn't been a successful archaeologist, he figured, maybe his teachers would have expected less from him.

"Why couldn't Dad be a taxi driver?" Alex complained to his younger sister, Cleo, as they ate lunch out in the quad.

"Why couldn't you actually pay attention in class?" Cleo countered.

"There's more chance of Dad being a taxi driver," Alex replied. He stuffed a sandwich into his mouth, swallowed a gulp of soda, tossed his carrot sticks onto his sister's lunch bag, and stood up. "Later."

Cleo watched her older brother race off. Lunch was always like this—Alex sitting with her just long enough to cram into his mouth what little food he'd brought before bolting off—and Cleo often wondered why he even spent that handful of minutes with her. She sat back in her wheelchair.

Cleo didn't have as many friends as Alex, but that never bothered her. She was a beauty, not that she knew it, with a sensitivity and awareness that contrasted with her sometimes stubborn, always determined nature. But being at the top of her class was hard work, and challenges were never something the fifteen-year-old girl backed away from. Life had given her many, and she had met them all head-on.

Cleo pushed herself away from the table and went looking around the cafeteria for her friend Jennie.

Alex had seen his friends Philip and Mike and immediately headed over.

"Check it out," Philip said to Alex, and slapped on a pair of glasses. They made his eyes look large and eerie, as if he'd been hypnotized by an evil magician.

"You are totally freaking me out with those," Alex said.

Philip took off the glasses. He held them out, and Alex saw that a photograph of an open eye was taped to the back of each lens.

"Now I can sleep in class and the teacher will totally think my eyes are still open. I just have to learn how to sleep sitting up." Philip was impressed by his own ingenuity. "Watch. I've been practicing."

Philip put the glasses back on and closed his eyes; the creepy eyes taped to the lenses glared out at Alex.

"That's the stupidest thing I've ever seen." Alex pulled the glasses off Philip's face and then reconsidered. "Never mind. You look better with them on."

Chapter Three

That night, Cleo's restful slumber was disturbed by a light knock on her door. Her left eye cracked open, slowly followed by her right.

"Hey, Dad," she mumbled.

"Hi, beauty," Dr. Bellows responded, staring at his daughter from the room's threshold.

"Do you need my help with the computer?" Cleo asked, noticing that it was the middle of the night.

Dr. Bellows smiled. Their roles were often reversed that way, parent turning to child for advice or support.

"No. Go back to sleep." He leaned over and gently kissed his daughter's forehead. His gesture of love betrayed his anxiety more than any word he might have spoken, but Cleo was too tired to notice his tension.

Dr. Bellows moved back to the hall and slowly closed the door. The door's shadow moved across the room like the sweeping hand of a giant clock. In its wake, darkness crept across Cleo, her bed, her nightstand, and finally her wheelchair, which waited patiently in the corner for its owner.

Across the hall, the newest batch of Alex's drawings covered his door, awaiting the admiration of any passerby like freshly mounted paintings in an art gallery.

Things had not been going as well between father and son as between father and daughter. The older Alex got, the more distant he seemed from Dr. Bellows. Now that he was seventeen, there were days when he didn't say any more to his father than "Hello."

"Am I late for school again?" Alex groggily muttered, his head stirring under his pillow.

"No. It's the middle of the night. Go back to sleep," Dr. Bellows replied, and ruffled Alex's hair.

"Dad?" Alex said. "Is that what you woke me up to tell me?"

Dr. Bellows stared at his son. "Pretty much."

Dr. Bellows entered his own bedroom and was surprised to find his wife, Lily Bellows, awake.

"You've got to stop that," she said the moment her husband appeared in the doorway.

"What?" Dr. Bellows feigned ignorance.

"Waking up the kids in the middle of the night."

"I wasn't . . . uh . . ."

"Coming to bed?"

Dr. Bellows ran his hand through his hair. "Got a couple of things to straighten out upstairs, and then, yeah, I will," he said, sighing.

"A good night's sleep wouldn't kill you. The CyberMuseum can wait."

Dr. Bellows offered Lily a smile, and she immediately knew everything her husband was thinking.

Lily returned his smile, and Dr. Bellows knew she understood. Tonight, the CyberMuseum would come first.

His wanderings through the house completed, Dr. Bellows made a quick stop in the kitchen for a sandwich and a tall glass of milk, then returned to the upstairs study.

"It's almost impossible for me to trust what I'm looking at," he said into the microphone.

As he spoke, the Gorgos Stone shimmered on the plasma screen, a digital reminder of the impossible. It had been twenty-four hours since he had scanned the stone into the CyberMuseum, and he had yet to discover a way to get it back out.

Dr. Bellows stopped and tapped the screen, wishing he could pull the cyberstone from the CyberMuseum.

"Image: delete."

The image of the Gorgos Stone didn't delete. Instead, it vibrated. A crack traversed its core, and a piercing blade of black light cut across the plasma screen. From the heart of the Gorgos Stone rose a shadow. Its shape was hard to define, vaguely human in form, yet somehow alien. Dr. Bellows watched it waver, then solidify into . . .

"Gorgos!" Dr. Bellows exploded at the screen, astounded. He was looking upon the mythic spirit of evil.

Freed from the Gorgos Stone after thousands of years, Gorgos burst forth with a tremendous scream of joy. The cry of *"Freedom! Freedom! Freedom!"* seemed to echo through the halls of the CyberMuseum.

Gorgos spun. The small statue of Cupid and Psyche caught his eye. Gorgos twisted his open hand and the statue shattered.

Gorgos laughed.

"Gorgos! I know who you are!" Dr. Bellows yelled at the screen as if suddenly waking from a hypnotic daze. "And you're supposed to be trapped inside your stone forever."

"It's too late now," Gorgos called out. "I'm free—and the gods who trapped me in that accursed stone will all come to regret it! I will have my revenge for what they did to me!"

Gorgos turned and pointed to five artifacts in quick succession. Each one exploded as if he had fired an invisible gun.

"No!" Dr. Bellows cried out, and instinctively reached for the screen. The instant his finger touched the shimmering Gorgos Stone, there was a flash of light.

Dr. Bellows was gone. The sandwich he had clenched in his left hand fell to the ground.

Gorgos's expression of triumph wilted into

one of shock. His stone collapsed on itself like a folding box and disappeared into nothingness.

"No!" Gorgos screamed. "Where is it? Where is my stone?"

Gorgos slammed his fist against a table. Muttered words passed between his gritted teeth, and then he too disappeared.

The empty study quickly filled with the over-whelming pressure of complete silence; the only signs that Dr. Matt Bellows had ever existed were a half-eaten sandwich and the broken pieces of the Ch'ang-o scattered across the table.

Chapter Four

The next morning, the elevator platform hummed to a stop at the top of the stairs. Cleo unlocked the wheels of her chair, then rolled into her father's empty study.

"Dad?" Of course, there was no answer.

"Computer: close CyberMuseum. Computer off."

The computer screen went black. Cleo paused for a moment and scanned the room. An icy chill flowed through her veins as she spotted her dad's half-eaten sandwich and the shattered pieces of the Ch'ang-o on the table.

Cleo spun her chair around with frightened urgency.

"Mom! Do you know where Dad went?" she called out, praying the answer would be yes.

Alex had a stomachache. His father was gone. Or maybe he wasn't gone. No one knew. There was no note, no message, nothing. Alex and Cleo had searched through the house while their mother called neighbors and friends. It felt as if their dad had simply vanished like a rabbit in a magic show.

"Normally, we don't consider it a missing persons case until they've been gone forty-eight hours," Detective Saybrook told Lily Bellows. "Especially a case like this: no evidence, no foul play. Nothing's missing—credit cards, money. Car's in the driveway."

"I'm not hiding him in the closet," Lily countered. She bit her lip for a moment, then finally realized what Detective Saybrook was implying. "You think he walked out on us!"

"It happens."

"Not in my house," Lily hissed back.

"People get lost," Detective Saybrook offered, hoping to curb Lily's growing anger.

"Not my dad," Alex said. "He's chopped his

way through jungles and wandered around places that would give you nightmares. He wouldn't get lost in suburbia!"

Before Alex could finish, Barbara Frazier burst into the room. "Omigod!" she yelled, then added, "Oh! My! God!" just to make certain everyone had heard. She raced to the broken pieces of the Ch'ang-o. "Don't touch it! Don't touch it!"

Alex watched and listened as his mother and Barbara Frazier got into an argument. "This won't find Dad!" he shouted after a moment, and stormed from the room.

"Computer: open CyberMuseum," Cleo commanded.

Barbara Frazier had returned with two men from Yale University. They'd collected all the crates full of artifacts that Dr. Bellows had brought home, then zoomed away in their truck. Now the study was tidy, almost sterile, and looked like a room in any house in any city—not like the study of Cleo's missing father.

The computer didn't respond. Cleo repeated the command, then manipulated the light mouse, with the same result.

"I hate computers!"

She tried the command a third time. The computer was still unwilling to cooperate. Cleo pulled open the bottom drawer of her dad's desk and slid out a small tool kit.

"We'll see who gets the last laugh," Alex heard his sister say as he passed the study on his way down the hall.

It had been three weeks since their dad's disappearance. Three long weeks of worry, tears, and uncertainty, and Alex had nothing to show for the sleepless nights and hours of searching but more questions.

The police had been little help. With no evidence of foul play, they had concluded that Dr. Bellows had simply left the family. Lily kept telling them how wrong they were. Something had happened to her husband, and it was not of his choice. But the only evidence she had to prove it was in her heart.

"That's not much for the police to go on," Detective Saybrook had said.

Alex left Cleo in the study and headed to his parents' bedroom. Once inside, he forgot why he had gone there, or whether he even had a reason at all. He wanted to look under the bed or in the closet, as if his dad were playing hide-and-seek and all Alex had to do was look a little harder. Alex plopped on the bed. He'd thought he felt helpless and lost when he took an algebra test, but no school exam had ever made him feel so empty.

"Hi," a voice behind him said. It was his mom. "What's up?"

"Nothing," Alex quickly replied, trying to cover his embarrassment. "I was just looking for . . . uh . . . something."

"For Dad? I know. I do it too," she said.

Alex started to protest but stopped. Why fight the truth? "We gonna be okay?" he finally asked.

Lily sat on the bed and patted a spot next to her for Alex to move over to. He looked around before he moved beside her, as if there might be someone hiding in the closet who would leap out once he began a heartfelt conversation with his mom.

"Alex, I know your father. I don't know what's going on, I don't know what happened, but I know he'll be back."

The words helped a little. Not a lot, but a little. Alex tried to smile but found that he couldn't.

"I know" was all he said.

Chapter Five

Alex and Cleo sat at a cafeteria bench. Alex slowly ate his sandwich, bite by bite. The days of devour and dash were a distant memory. He now spent every minute of lunch hanging out with his sister.

Alex didn't know why, but since their dad had disappeared, he found himself wanting to spend more time with his mom and Cleo, almost as if continuing to grow apart from them—as he had been doing with his father—would make them disappear too.

"We could check the Internet for a missing persons database . . . ," Alex began, breaking the silence the moment the thought occurred to him.

"Did it," Cleo responded.

"How about posters, ads, e-mails, talk shows . . . God, Cleo, there must be something we can do besides sitting in English class every day!"

"I know. It's driving me crazy too," Cleo agreed.

The two watched the students out on the quad. Some were laughing, others were lounging, two were kissing. It didn't matter—all of them seemed like aliens to Alex, aliens who had no idea how lucky they were.

Alex remembered that it wasn't that long ago that he'd been lucky too.

"You know, Alex, sometimes at night I just wake up and hope Dad's standing at my door, checking up on me like he used to," Cleo confessed.

"I know, Cleo. I never thought I'd miss that, but I do." Alex smiled at his sister. "You know what I think about the most? The stupid things. Like the time I got that D and Dad grounded me for a week. Y'know, I didn't talk to him for that whole time. How idiotic was that?"

"Don't be so hard on yourself. You didn't know Dad would disappear. You just thought he'd still be there when you weren't mad anymore."

"But he's not here, Cleo. He's not. And no matter what we try, we can't do anything about it. I hate it!"

Cleo took a deep breath. Alex's frustration matched her own. "I've been thinking, I should call Barbara at Yale. Maybe she can give me a list of Dad's archaeological associates. Maybe they might be able to help."

"Yeah, yeah. Do that. I'll call and talk to them. You see what you can find out about all of them on the Internet. Who knows. I mean, maybe Dad had an enemy or something," Alex answered.

"You don't think . . ."

"I don't know what to think, Cleo."

The bell rang. Alex stood up from the table. He walked at his sister's side to the hall across the quad; then they went their separate ways toward the next class.

Alex reached the corner. He stopped and

looked back at his sister one more time, as if he wanted to make sure she was still there.

She was.

Alex grabbed the classroom door, then stopped. Why sit in class another day? "What's the point?" he wondered aloud.

"Are you going in or what?" It was Philip.

Alex let go of the handle. "Nah. You wanna do something else?"

"What do you think?"

"I was thinking of going to the library," Alex suggested.

"The place with the books?"

"Yeah."

"Do they have a TV there?" Philip asked hopefully.

"No."

"And you still want to go?"

"Yeah. I want to get on the Net. Check some police databases from other states."

Philip looked through the window. Mr. Watt was handing sheets of paper to the students. "The library?" Philip asked again.

"Come on, Philip. I could use the company," Alex said.

Philip smiled at his friend and the two headed off.

. . .

An hour later Alex and Philip emerged from the library. Philip had actually tried to read a book, while Alex had passed the time surfing the Net, looking for a lead, a hint, a clue, researching anything that could shed light on what might have happened to his dad.

"Well, if you were hiding from me, the library would certainly be the last place I would ever look for you two," Mr. Watt said, spotting the two class-ditchers in the hall. "Why weren't you in class today? We had a test."

"That's why we weren't in class, then," Philip joked.

Alex stepped in front of Philip before he could cause more trouble.

"We're real sorry, Mr. Watt. We forgot. Honest. It won't happen again." Alex was looking for something to compliment Mr. Watt about before he dazzled him with his charm.

"Don't even think about complimenting my tie," Mr. Watt interrupted as Alex opened his mouth.

Alex was about to speak again.

"Or my shoes," Mr. Watt cut in.

"Look, I'll tell you what," Alex began, shifting his strategy. "It's Friday. Let's all just have a great weekend and we'll just have a makeup test on Monday."

"Oh, we will, will we?" Mr. Watt raised an eyebrow.

"Please?"

"Makeup test on Monday, extra-credit history paper due on Wednesday," Mr. Watt responded.

"Makeup test on Monday, current events report on Friday," Alex countered.

"Deal."

Chapter Six

Cleo had taken her dad's computer apart and tested each chip, every board, and all the circuits. After hours and hours of labor, she was certain of only one thing: She had no idea why the computer wouldn't work.

She tightened the final screw. She was stumped.

"Computer: on," she said, though doubting anything would happen. It hadn't before, she hadn't fixed any problem, so why should it work now?

But it did.

The screen flashed on, and within seconds the boot was completed and the CyberMuseum doors appeared before her stunned eyes.

"Um . . . let's try . . . open: India—fabrics," Cleo said into the microphone.

There was rapid movement down five hallways and around six corners, and before Cleo could take another breath, she was staring speechless at the center of the India Room.

"I don't understand," she said aloud. "Why is it suddenly working?"

She was even more amazed at the vibrancy and richness of the images before her. The collection of Indian saris and silks featured in the India Room seemed to have a life they had never shown before. Colors collided with texture to form surfaces so realistic, Cleo nearly reached out to pluck them from the screen.

"Computer: show installer log," she ordered, thinking her father might have installed new software to get such brilliant definition.

INSTALLER LOG EMPTY flashed on the screen.

Cleo scratched her head. Maybe she had damaged the hard drive during her repairs. Or maybe . . .

Her eyes widened.

. . .

Alex sat in the middle of a mountain of dishes, pastas, sauces, spoons, vegetables, slicers, dicers, shredders, pots, pans, and one tub of butter.

Lily was cooking.

Her busy catering business kept their kitchen in constant use—and their refrigerator fully stocked with everything from hors d'oeuvres to fancy desserts.

While Lily stirred and cut, poured and measured, Alex quietly finished off another elaborate drawing. He had been drawing more since his dad's disappearance. Getting lost in the curves and shadows of his sketches was a better option than worrying and grieving.

"Alex! You've got to come see this!" Cleo's sudden call from the doorway shattered the shared solitude of Lily and Alex in the kitchen.

"What?" Alex asked, looking up from his drawing.

"It's important. Just come upstairs." Cleo widened her eyes, as if to say, "It's also important that Mom doesn't know."

Alex dragged himself away from the delicious chaos in the kitchen and joined his sister upstairs.

"Okay, what?" he growled at her.

"Come here," she responded eagerly.

"What's got you so wonked out?"

"Just look," Cleo said, then rolled back a few feet to give Alex a clear view of the screen.

Alex sighed and moved closer. "What is it? A new urn?" he asked sarcastically. "I know! It's a Neanderthal digging tool!"

Alex was shocked that no such trivial item greeted him. He studied the CyberMuseum objects, each real enough to touch.

"The room! Everything's so real," he said excitedly. "Talk about your tight graphics. Dad did something to the program he never showed me."

"No way he did this. Not without me knowing," Cleo assured him. "And I already checked. No new installs."

"The CyberMuseum's bursting with color. So what?"

"This is one of your basic down-to-earth, in-your-face, hey-look-at-me *clues*," Cleo said with deep satisfaction.

"That's a clue?" he asked. "I admit the room looks weird, like it's real. Man, it totally feels like I could just grab something off the screen."

"If you do, grab Dionysus. It's worth a fortune," Cleo joked.

"That guy?" Alex asked, motioning toward the figure molded in the center of a golden pendant. "Isn't he the god of wine or something?"

"One and the same," Cleo confirmed.

"Come here, my little baby! Make Alex a rich man!" Alex laughed, and reached for the screen. His middle finger brushed against the virtual image of Dionysus and then . . .

Zap!

It wasn't so much a flash of light as an implosion—a soundless, instantaneous moment between existence and oblivion.

Before Cleo could blink, her brother was gone.

Chapter Seven

"Alex! Alex!" Cleo shouted at the computer. One moment her brother had been sitting next to her, reaching out for the plasma screen, and the next moment he was—

Cleo's eyes locked on the screen before her. Nothing she had ever experienced in her life could have prepared her for what she saw.

Alex was on the screen.

Alex spun around. Whatever confusion Cleo felt, it was multiplied by ten for Alex. He had just been sitting in the study with Cleo, and now he lay under an azure sky. A warm breeze brushed his skin. He was certain he was dreaming.

"Alex!"

Alex heard his sister's voice and looked for her. It sounded as if she were standing next to him, but she was nowhere to be seen.

"Cleo?" he asked tentatively, not sure whether he had really heard anything. "Is that you? I can hear you!"

"Bull!" Cleo's voice shouted.

"No, I can!" Alex grew excited. It was definitely his sister.

"No, Alex! Bull! Behind you!" Cleo's disembodied voice warned.

Alex followed the prompting of Cleo's voice and turned to see a massive, angry bull—at the exact moment when it plowed headfirst into his gut. Alex tumbled to the ground, pain shooting through his ribs and stomach.

This was no dream.

Knocked over backward, Alex took a moment to catch his breath and finally noticed his surroundings. He was in an arena. A crowd of thousands shouted and cheered from behind the stone walls. Alex quickly noticed that their clothing looked like something from a

Hollywood gladiator movie. The wooden seats of the coliseum rocked with the exuberant crowd. A din of trumpets and horns echoed like man-made thunder. The fans clamored for more, the same way Alex often did from the bleachers after a home run. They wanted entertainment, and Alex quickly realized that he was the show.

Am I on a movie set? Alex wondered. *This place is crazy!*

Alex didn't care whether he was in the Palace of Knossos in ancient Crete or Yankee Stadium in New York. A second bull was charging at him, its horns lowered to the level of Alex's head.

Alex jumped up and tried to dodge. He narrowly avoided the horns, but the bull's head caught him in the side again and sent him back into the dirt.

"This is worse than a math final," Alex groaned.

Enough was enough. Bull or no, Alex was tired of being smashed in the gut. He stepped backward to put distance between him and the animals. That was when he realized that these were no animals—or at least they weren't bulls.

They were men. Three of them, to be exact,

each wearing an oversized bull's head. They wore leather sandals and leather loincloths. Behind the bull-men a whole parade of people—priests, soldiers, musicians, dancers—spoke a litany of prayers, stood at attention, played their instruments, or danced wildly with the fury of a bottled tempest.

"What is going on?" Alex called out to Cleo.

"You're in the computer!" Cleo's voice called back.

"Thanks for the info. That really helps." Alex didn't mean to be impatient, but he'd been hoping for an answer that would prevent him from getting his butt kicked.

He touched his ribs and grimaced. Nothing felt broken, but it sure hurt. Bruises would come tomorrow. He just hoped he would live long enough to see them.

The third bull-man raced toward Alex amid the cheers of the crowd. Alex was ready this time, and he prepared to fight.

"This way! Over here!" Alex heard a voice behind him call out.

Help? Alex wondered. On this day of amazing impossibilities, anything could happen.

Alex saw several people waving to him from

behind a safety wall. The bull was almost upon him, and Alex turned and fled.

The crowd erupted with laughter, but Alex didn't care. *Let's see how funny they think it is after they get plowed over by one of these nuts,* he thought.

The bull-man was almost on top of him. It would be close. Getting hit in the stomach was bad enough. Alex didn't want to even consider taking a horn in the back, but he had little choice in the matter, as the bull-man was about to plant a horn in his spine.

Chapter Eight

Alex vaulted the safety wall and crashed into
the arms of apparent friends. The bull-man was
not so lucky and plowed headfirst into the wall.
The bull-man crumpled to the ground and the
crowd erupted with humiliating laughter.

"At least they laugh at anything," Alex said to
no one in particular.

He quickly found himself surrounded by
several young Athenians, who eagerly offered
him congratulations and tended to his ribs.

Alex was thankful for the friendly faces but
still had no idea what was happening.

"I'm okay. I'm okay," he assured them.

One young woman named Leto stepped forward. Like the people in the crowd, she wore a simple white tunic and sandals. Her blond hair hung from her head in thick curls, a single lock hanging down toward her blue eyes.

"It didn't look like you were doing too well," she said to Alex.

"Let's see how *you* do against those three nuts. This is worse than *Rage in the Cage*! Would someone tell me what is going on? Where am I? Who are—"

The others seemed to be ignoring Alex's questions. The woman—Alex heard someone call her Leto—took a step closer to Alex, seeming overly concerned with his well-being.

"Could you just back off a minute?" Alex insisted, waving his hands.

Leto stepped away instantly as if Alex's request were a command. He looked down and saw that he was wearing the same style of garb as these prisoners, but his tunic was more ornate, his sandals made of newer leather. A golden belt was wrapped around his waist, rather than a length of rope like the others'.

"Cleo! Cleo?" Alex whispered.

"God, Alex, what's going on?" he heard Cleo's voice asking.

"That is the last thing I wanted to hear from you!" Alex moaned. Even though he had retreated to the corner, the other Athenians watched him closely.

Their looks were ones of uncertainty and concern. Finally a young man cracked a smile and turned to his companions.

"What's he doing, Philitas?" Leto asked the young man.

"Ah! He's talking to the gods," Philitas reasoned. "Either that or he's crazy."

"I'm having a nightmare, right?" Alex pleaded with Cleo.

"Only if we dream in sync, because I'm having it too."

"You can see me?" Alex asked, then looked up, almost expecting to see Cleo looking down on him like the distant gods of whom Philitas spoke.

"I can see everything right on Dad's plasma screen," Cleo confirmed.

"Am I in the computer?" Alex called out.

"No. I see you on the screen . . . but I think you're in ancient Greece."

"I think you're right." Alex's reply had a hint of fear.

Alex heard the roar of the crowd. He peeked around the safety wall. The pageantry of the bull-men, dancers, musicians, soldiers, and priests continued, much to the pleasure of the crowd. The parade moved about the ring like orbiting planets, and Alex wondered what was the point of the ritual.

"We're all going to die," Leto said, appearing at Alex's shoulder.

So *that* was the point.

Alex saw no reason to reply as he noticed two spear-carrying soldiers coming toward the safety wall.

"Of course we're going to die," a youth named Kadilus stated as plainly as if he were ordering scrambled eggs. "That was true the minute they put us on the boat in Athens and sent us here." There was nothing about this man's garb or manner that made him stand out from the other young men and women who gathered around Alex again. His hair was as black as Philitas's, and the same dark eyes stared out from his boyish face. But there was something about him that didn't seem right. Alex didn't have time to worry about that now, though.

"What do you mean, die!" Alex spat, peeling his eyes away from the approaching soldiers. "Some guy in a bull mask is gonna kill us? I did not come here to die."

"Easy for you to say," Philitas said. "Look at you . . . look at us."

Alex wasn't sure what the comment meant, but he did know his throat was dry and burning. He leaned over a water barrel to drink and saw his reflection. Unbelievable! He totally understood what Philitas meant.

Alex wasn't Alex. His reflection was that of a young man more than six feet tall, with thick brown hair. His face appeared gentle and kind, in stark contrast to the fierce muscles of his chiseled body. Broad shoulders filled his elegant tunic, and the rest of his powerful body flowed beneath like molded steel. Muscles rippled under the fine cloth, and Alex suddenly felt that he could beat any trio of bull-headed men.

Is that really me? Alex wondered. When he moved, the reflection moved. Alex turned around. There was no one behind him. He leaned toward the water, squinting at his unbelievable physique.

"Always room for vanity with you Athenians," a voice said.

Alex looked up and realized that two soldiers stood over him.

One of the soldiers poked Alex with his spear. "Hey!" Alex protested.

"You're so brave?" Kadilus began in his monotonous voice. "Go on and show them what Athenians are made of."

"A bucket of blood and some broken bones," the soldier who had poked Alex quipped.

Alex lost interest in his reflection, impressive or otherwise, the moment he realized that the soldiers had come to take him back out into the arena. Once more the soldier poked him with his spear.

"Hey!" Alex protested again. "Is that really necessary? Can't you go jab someone else?"

"These Cretans," Philitas sneered. "Always poking things with sticks."

"You forget," Kadilus offered sleepily, "the rest of us had no choice about coming here. But you, you volunteered. It's time to let them see why."

"I volunteered? No way!"

A hush fell. Even the two soldiers looked perplexed.

"No . . . way . . . ?" One of them asked, unsure what the expression meant.

"Yes, way. I think he's right," Cleo suddenly cut in. Alex could tell by the nonresponse of the others in the small room that he was the only one who could hear Cleo's voice.

"You telling me I'm bull fodder?" Alex grumbled.

"Give me a second here, I'm looking you up." Cleo grabbed a stack of her father's research books.

Having lost patience with Alex and his odd behavior, a soldier stepped forward and delivered a hard jab with the blunt end of his spear.

"Stop that!" Alex yelled, and swatted at him as if he had just been stung by a mischievous bee. Alex turned to Kadilus and the others. "I thought we were all buds here. Isn't someone going to speak up? Isn't somebody going to do something!" he pleaded.

"I will!" Philitas stepped forward from the group. He walked over to Alex and patted him on the back. "Good luck."

"What did the gods tell you?" Leto asked.

"The gods? What gods?" Alex was confused. Maybe even more so than the group of Athenians who were now whispering about their leader's inexplicable behavior.

One of the soldiers raised his spear again, and Alex took a step toward the arena.

"Ever hear the expression 'horns of a dilemma'?" Alex asked Kadilus, hoping for even the smallest diversion.

"I'd be worrying more about the *Minotaur's* horns if I were you," the soldier growled.

"The Minotaur!" Cleo shouted. "That's it! You're in a myth!"

"*In* a myth? You're crazy," Alex countered. "There's no such thing as a Minotaur."

"There is *there*. All this is straight out of the myth of Theseus."

"If this is real, how did I get here?" Alex questioned.

"You touched the plasma screen. Something like this must've happened to Dad," Cleo reasoned.

"Do the gods have a plan?" Leto asked Alex anxiously.

"A—a plan?" Alex stammered. These people thought he was talking to gods? Maybe Cleo was right after all. "A plan. Yeah . . . yeah!" Alex had used his charm on his mom and dad many times with smashing success. Sure, there had been times when he'd failed, but those were few. Besides, Alex reasoned, these were practically Stone Age people. They already seemed to idolize him. He should have them eating out of his hand in no time.

"The gods. Yes. A plan," Alex continued. "The gods said that if we go out there one at a time, we're all dead—"

"And they figured that out all by themselves?" Philitas groaned.

"But . . . ," Alex said. He was working up a head of steam. "But if we stick together, we have a chance!"

"How?" Leto demanded.

"For starters . . ." Alex paused. Here came the sell, the one sentence that would make or break him. "I don't go out there alone. We all go!"

"I sure didn't see that one coming," Philitas remarked.

If Alex had had a pin to drop, he would have been able to hear it bounce on the dirt floor.

"The gods said this?" Leto's doubtful tone was matched by her unbelieving expression.

"They sure did," Alex replied with a surge of glee. He looked at the blank faces. "Are you with me?" he added, sounding like a cheerleader in his bravado.

"Of course we're with you!" Philitas shouted, then added, "We're with you all the way to the door."

The soldier let out a sigh of anger and jabbed Alex one last time toward the arena. Alex stumbled forward and was instantly blanketed by the surging roar of the crowd.

The three bull-men stood waiting. One shouted and kicked at the dirt like a real bull ready to charge. Alex's heart pounded in his chest with such power, he was surprised it didn't drown out the blood-hungry shouts of the crowd.

Alex looked back over his shoulder. Leto and Kadilus peered around the safety wall for a brief instant.

"So who's with me?" Alex called back, although he already knew that the answer was, apparently, no one.

"Don't forget to make a funny noise when the bull-man gouges you!" Philitas advised from behind the safety wall. "That's always a crowd-pleaser!"

That was when the bull-man Alex had caused

to crash into the wall charged. He raced head-long toward the defenseless Alex, hungry to erase the humiliation of the earlier encounter, hungry for revenge, hungry to feel his horns dig deep into Alex's chest.

Chapter Nine

"**Die!**" **the bull-man** screamed. He charged at Alex, head down, legs churning fast on the floor of the arena.

I wish I'd taken those karate classes, Alex thought. He knew nothing about hand-to-hand combat except some tips he'd picked up playing video games. *But I doubt there are any "power-up" items around here,* he thought.

Alex waited, partly out of fear, but partly because the beginnings of a new plan were rattling around in his head. The bull-man lunged at

Alex, pointed horns catching the light of the burning noon sun. Alex quickly sidestepped, leaving his right foot in the bull-man's path.

The attacker tripped over Alex's foot and crashed into the dirt facefirst. The ground shook from the collision of bull-man and earth. Dust filled the air. That was all Alex needed. He zipped across the arena like a nimble running back heading toward the goal line.

"Crazy bull-man or not, the old 'have a good trip, see you next fall' always works!" Alex called out to Cleo.

The crowd roared. They joyfully basked in every prolonged minute of the spectacle. They laughed and pointed at the bull-men. How easy it had been for the man from Athens to embarrass them! The crowd had not seen entertainment like this in Crete for a long time. Usually a fight in the arena ended in minutes as the bull-men made quick work of their opponents. But this promised to last possibly fifteen or thirty minutes—or at least until the fighter grew weary.

Alex stopped running, leaning against the wall of the arena to catch his breath. He smiled slightly, but he knew there was really nothing to be happy about. It wasn't over yet. Not even close.

Alex looked up. The bull-men were running his way.

"Great. The new Three Stooges are back," Alex said between deep breaths.

"This is not how it is supposed to be!" High above the arena, an angry King Minos stomped around in the royal box. With his gray beard and golden crown, he could be spotted in a crowd with ease. He ruled Crete with an iron fist, and he wanted everything to go his way.

"Why doesn't he stand his ground and fight?" King Minos bellowed. "He's making a mockery of us all!"

"Well, sir," a lackey commented, "the crowd does seem to be enjoying it."

The king glared at the lackey, who quickly backed out of the royal box. It would be several weeks before he dared to speak to the king again.

"And mock us he should, Father!"

Princess Ariadne, the king's beautiful daughter, stood at her father's side. She leaned over the royal box, unable to take her eyes off Alex. "This pageant . . . this tradition . . . it's terrible!"

"You would be wise to hold your tongue, daughter," King Minos warned. "The gods have cursed us once already."

"And we will stay cursed as long as you allow these 'games' to continue."

Ariadne wanted to leave. She hated it when her father made her watch these events. But this time it was different. This time more than her sympathy went out to the Athenian fighting in the arena. This time, her heart went out as well. Ariadne had never seen anyone like Alex as Theseus before, and, at that moment, she swore to do all she could to aid him.

Back in the arena, the creatures surrounded Alex, stepping carefully, deliberately. Despite their size, they had a certain grace, like the sumo wrestlers of Japan.

"Alex! I think I figured it out." It was Cleo's voice ringing in his head.

"That's great. But I'm a little busy right now," he replied. "Hey!"

The first creature was upon him. He grabbed Alex by his shoulders. Alex hit him back.

"How do *you* like it?" Alex yelled.

The creature yanked Alex off the ground,

twisted him into the air, then body-slammed him to the ground.

The bull-man rose, lifting his arms into the air in victory. The crowd roared its approval. *One minute they love me, the next they love him better,* Alex thought. *Fame.*

The second bull-man moved in. Alex tried rolling out of the way, but the creature smacked him with his right forearm. He picked up the stunned Alex by his tunic and hurled him through the air.

"Tuck and roll! Tuck and roll!" Cleo screamed through the computer.

Alex hit the ground and rolled to the wall, gasping for breath. Slowly he stood up. Legs still worked. Back was in one piece. No broken bones. Then he saw the third bull-man coming straight at him.

Alex glanced around furtively, anxiously. He was trapped. This was it, unless . . . he caught sight of the royal banner draped across the wall behind him.

Come on, Alex! Alex commanded himself. *Think! Think! There must be something I can use to—*

Alex's hand shot up and he grabbed the banner, ripping it from the wall. He took two steps toward the creature and waved the banner like a matador's red cape. The creature ran toward him. Closer. Closer.

Now!

Alex quickly jumped to the side and wrapped the banner around the bull-man's head. Blinded, the bull-man plowed into the wall, smacking his head at full speed. The arena wall cracked like a frail egg. The bull-man slowly crumpled to the ground, unconscious.

The crowd registered its approval with loud cheers. Alex could see the safety pit at the side of the arena. Leto and Philitas cheered as well.

"He is doing well!" Leto said. "Bravo!"

"There are still two bull-men left," Kadilus reminded her.

In the arena, Alex tugged the banner from his unconscious opponent and waved it at the other two, taunting them. "Larry had his turn. I guess it's time for Moe and Curly. Come and get me, boys!" he yelled.

The two bull-men stopped in the center of the arena. They ripped off their bull heads and threw them to the ground. They had had enough of this game. In a fury, they drew their swords from the scabbards at their sides and charged toward Alex.

"Prepare to die, Athenian dog!"

Terror shot through Alex and froze him to the ground. He dropped the banner—no cloth could save him from the cold steel and hatred coming his way.

Chapter Ten

The swords.

That was all Alex saw.

The crowds, the bull-men, his companions, they were lost to him behind the dizzying images of two swords swinging against the blue sky. One bull-man raised his sword sharply above his head and readied himself to make the final blow.

"Stay your swords!" King Minos's voice blared from the royal box, filling the arena. The former bull-men stopped, the tips of their blades a hair away from Alex's heart.

King Minos waved in the direction of the safety pit. Three of his soldiers herded the rest of the Athenians into the arena at blade point. They all stood next to Alex, below King Minos's royal box.

"Every nine years," King Minos began, "as punishment for the death of my son at their hands, Athens is required to pay a tribute to me. Ten of their most promising youths are sent here as a sacrifice to the Minotaur."

Minos pointed to the crowd around Alex and continued. "But these embarrass me greatly. They are an insult to the great Minotaur. I am outraged."

"And you're nuts!" Alex yelled back. "What are you doing to us? You've got no right to—"

Alex's rant was quickly drowned out by the flooding boos and hisses of the crowd. At Minos's left stood Princess Ariadne. Alex had never seen anyone so beautiful—she was ravishing, with her dark, curly hair and piercing eyes. She stared at Alex with more than casual interest. Or so it seemed to him.

"Who is *that*?" Alex whispered to Leto.

"That's Princess Ariadne," Leto replied. "The king's daughter. Don't even think about it."

But Alex didn't really hear the warning. And he was oblivious to the taunts and jeers of the crowd. He was busy staring at Ariadne with the same intensity with which she was staring at him.

"Today is merely a diversion," Minos said. "These prisoners are here to forfeit their lives, and forfeit them they will. Tomorrow they will face their gods and try to explain."

The crowd registered its approval of the king's remarks by standing and cheering. Minos took time to enjoy his moment in the spotlight.

"Alex!" It was Cleo again, ringing in Alex's head.

"This is not a good time," Alex whispered, but Philitas had overheard.

"Are you talking to the gods again?" he whispered to Alex. "Ask them for some better sandals. These are killing my feet."

"It's more like a pestering spirit," Alex retorted.

"I heard that!" Cleo said.

Before Alex could continue his conversation with his little sister, Minos pointed to him.

"This year we have among us a young hero who boasts that he will best the Minotaur with his bare hands. But I doubt it. Certainly not with the skills he showed us here today. This man is the royal prince, Theseus, son of my enemy, King Aegeus."

"If I didn't know better," Alex whispered to Leto, "I'd think he was pointing right at me!"

"He *is* pointing at you," Leto replied.

"Because you *are* Theseus!" Cleo yelled into his head.

"Me!" Alex said aloud. "He wants me to fight the Minotaur?"

It was King Minos who replied. "We have kept the beast especially hungry, just for you, Theseus."

Alex looked at his new friends, Leto, Kadilus, and Philitas. They shook their heads in sympathy.

"Don't worry, Theseus, I know you'll kill the Minotaur," Philitas said enthusiastically, but quickly added to himself, "If he chokes to death on your rib bone."

"Alex! That's what I've been trying to tell you!" Cleo screamed excitedly. "You haven't traveled to the past! You're trapped in a myth! There's a Minotaur in a labyrinth and you're going to have to kill it."

A great roar echoed through the arena,

stilling the crowd. Horrible, agonizing, unearthly, the roar had come from behind the doors of the labyrinth, rattling the very doors that kept it a prisoner.

The Minotaur. The real one.

The players in the pageant shuddered in fear and moved away from the arena as quickly as they could. This was a game no longer. Fear swept through the arena and killed the cheers, destroyed the splendor, and shot a chill through Alex's pounding heart.

"Did you hear that?" Alex whispered to Cleo. "What do I do now?"

Aroused by the harrowing roar, the unconscious bull-man stumbled to his feet. He was still wobbly and moving slowly. He tried clumsily to remove his bull's-head mask.

"Our Athenian guests need to know that the real Minotaur is not a playful pageant such as we have seen here today. He is not only real, he is deadly and hungry." Minos pointed two fingers toward the unsteady bull-man.

Three soldiers rushed in and grabbed the unfortunate one. His bull's head rolled off as they dragged him away, toward the great doors under the royal box. The man screamed, but it might as well have been a hoarse whisper. If anyone heard it, no one cared.

Four large men opened the great doors to the labyrinth, and as they did, another horrific roar burst forth from the passages beyond. Alex had never heard a sound like it.

The man was shoved into the entranceway, and the mighty doors were shut and locked behind him. Momentary silence was shattered by another roar, then another, and then a scream of sheer terror came from the man trapped inside.

Then there was nothing but silence. The Minotaur had fed.

"Your time will come tomorrow, Theseus," King Minos said. "Sleep well tonight." He turned and made his royal exit. Princess Ariadne followed, turning back for one last look at Alex.

Chapter Eleven

"Ouch! Watch it!" Alex yelped in pain.

"Sorry!" Leto said. "But your muscles are very tense. That was quite a show today."

Leto massaged Alex's shoulders as if he were a prizefighter before a championship bout. During the massage, Alex sketched with a piece of charcoal on a sheet of papyrus.

Down in the safety pit, which was really their prison, the Athenians were glum. Despite their "victory" in the arena that day, they could still hear the occasional roar of the Minotaur through the walls.

"Brave Theseus, think of it as fighting a real bull," Philitas rationalized. "If a bull were twelve feet tall and crazy and ate human flesh."

Leto kept working on Alex's shoulders. There was some bruising, but fortunately nothing was broken.

"The Minotaur is not human and not animal," Kadilus said, finally showing a hint of emotion. "He is the worst of both. He's a genuine monster."

"I heard it has two heads!" Philitas offered. "And huge claws that can shred a body into pieces. Bite-sized pieces."

The others nodded in silent agreement. They had heard similar stories of the Minotaur and its deadly abilities. They had all lost family and friends to King Minos's sacrifices.

"Whatever kind of creature it is—four-legged, ten-eyed, sharp claws, pointed fangs, twenty feet tall with the strength of a hundred men—it is of no consequence." Leto patted Alex's back. "Theseus will kill it quickly and free Athens and our people from these sacrifices forever. Am I right?"

Alex didn't respond, but he had finished his sketch, a terrific likeness of his father. He held it out to Leto and the others.

"Have you seen this man anywhere? If not here, maybe back in Athens?" The hope in Alex's voice disappeared as he saw the blank faces of the Athenians.

Leto shook her head and passed the sketch around. "He doesn't look familiar," she said. "But he may have come to Athens after we left."

"Is he a friend of yours?" Kadilus asked, cocking an eyebrow.

"A distant relative," Alex replied. "Very distant right now." *Distant and alone and he may not even look like himself anymore,* Alex thought. After all, the Athenians thought Alex looked just like Theseus.

Alex took back the drawing and folded it inside his tunic for safekeeping. He looked at his new friends, the ones who were pinning their hopes, their freedom, and their lives on his skills. If only they knew. Alex wasn't Theseus. He doubted he could beat up the school bully, let alone a man-eater like the Minotaur.

But Alex had no time to dwell further on his identity or his fate. The doors burst open and three guards shoved their way into the room at sword point.

"Theseus, Prince of Athens," one of the guards roared, and pointed at Alex.

Alex stepped forward. There was certainly no use denying it. After all, he did look like Theseus, and how could he ever explain that he was just Alex Bellows, from twenty-first-century Earth, trapped in a myth and looking for his father? Even if they understood the words, would they know their meaning? Would it make any difference?

"Yes," Alex agreed.

"Come with us." The guards grabbed Alex and ushered him away.

"Where are you taking him?" Leto demanded. The guard shoved her aside and shut the door, sliding the bolt to secure it.

Alex would have liked to know as well, but the guards didn't look as if they were in the mood for conversation. They led Alex through a series of hallways, chambers, and stairwells without a word. All Alex heard was the sound of their footsteps on the stone floor.

They finally stopped in front of a pair of ornate doors, the kind Alex had seen only in movies. One of the guards knocked on the doors, then pushed them open. Alex saw a large room, brightly decorated with floor-to-ceiling murals of sea creatures and bull dancers, pictures of parties and festivals, but also scenes of war and destruction.

The guards led Alex to the center of the room and left him there.

"Wait here and don't move," their leader ordered. "We'll be right outside."

They closed the door behind them as they left. Alex was alone.

Chapter Twelve

"Alex! I've been waiting for them to leave you alone." Or almost alone. As long as Cleo was on the other side of the plasma screen at their father's computer, he was never truly alone. "I've gone through a ton of Dad's mythology texts, checking and rechecking my facts."

"Okay. What have you found? Can you get me out of here?"

"We need to talk, but Mom's been calling me for the last five minutes, so I've got to run soon or she'll come up here." Cleo sat at the plasma screen, the reference books piled high around her. She could hear her mother calling her from downstairs. "Are you okay?" Cleo asked her brother.

"What do you mean?" Alex asked in reply. "Do I look scared to you? I'm fine. Really."

"I didn't ask if you were scared," Cleo corrected him. "Are you *okay*?"

"Yeah. So far. Where am I?"

"According to my research, you're on Crete. In Knossos. And you've got to get out of there as quickly as possible. You're in terrible danger."

"Okay. Point me in the direction of the nearest bus stop. How about a subway station? Or an airport? I'm not picky right now." After Alex had gotten the sarcasm out of his system, he added, "This is nuts, Cleo. I can't have time-traveled to ancient Crete, and there's no such thing as a Minotaur."

"That is where you are," Cleo said. "I don't think you're in ancient Crete, the historical one. Everything that's happening to you is right out of the myth of Theseus."

"So if it's not real, how did I get here?"

"I don't really understand the technology of it," Cleo replied. "All you did was touch the computer screen. Dad must have done something similar and that's what happened to him, too."

Alex was relieved, somewhat. That meant that their father might still be alive, just trapped somewhere in the computer, in this myth or another or . . .

"Okay, then how do I get out?"

Cleo shook her head. "I don't know that, either. What I do know is that you have to keep your wits about you. This is a dangerous time for Theseus."

Cleo heard her mother's voice again. "I've gotta go. If I don't go downstairs, Mom's going to bring my dinner up here."

"Don't let her! She can't see me like this—she can't know about Dad."

"I know. I'll be back." Cleo wheeled her chair away from the computer.

"Okay, but hurry. And whatever you do, don't turn off the computer! Okay? Cleo?" There was only silence. "Please?"

With Cleo gone, Alex was truly alone. He looked around the room. It certainly wasn't a cell—it was too well decorated for that. There was a large bed in the center of one wall. And not a normal bed, either. It looked like a bed reserved for royalty. Maybe there was a weapon somewhere, or something that could be used as a weapon. Anything to give him an edge against whatever he was waiting for.

Alex searched the room but found nothing. Nothing useful, anyway. That was when he heard the voices in the hallway. The door opened, and Alex turned to see Princess Ariadne. She entered the room alone, staring at him.

She was beautiful, positively radiant. Alex had never seen a girl so attractive, so compelling. She shut the door behind her and locked it.

"Finally!" she squealed. She ran toward Alex, threw her arms around him, and embraced him with a passionate kiss.

Alex was at a loss. A beautiful woman—a princess!—was kissing him. This wasn't like any myth he'd read about. Princess Ariadne relaxed her grip on Alex's body, and her lips slid from his.

"Princess, what . . . ?" Alex was so startled he couldn't finish his sentence.

"Shhh! You're here, Theseus, and that's all that matters." Ariadne clapped her hands, and two women entered the royal bedchamber carrying a large woman's tunic.

"Hey, what's going on?"

"It's just a dress," Ariadne explained. "It won't kill you. I wear one all the time."

She did, and she looked great in hers, Alex thought. "Okay, the dress won't kill me, but the Minotaur will, Princess. I don't have time to play dress-up with you."

"Please, you don't understand, Theseus. You're the only one who can kill my brother."

"B-brother?" The thought was so shocking, Alex stumbled on the word.

"That's right," Cleo said, hunched over the plasma screen, back in their father's study after dinner. "The Minotaur is her brother. It seems the god Poseidon sent King Minos a great white bull to sacrifice, but it was so beautiful, the king decided to keep it for himself. Poseidon wasn't happy, so he punished Minos."

Alex was listening to his little sister as Ariadne's ladies-in-waiting slipped the tunic over his head. He looked in the mirror. He would've liked a nice pair of jeans, an old T-shirt, and some sneakers better, but what choice did he have?

"Nice dress," Cleo chuckled, then continued. "Poseidon had the queen, Minos's wife and

Ariadne's mom, fall in love with the bull. Drinks, dinner, soft music, one thing led to another. You get the idea. After the baby was born and Minos saw that it was a monster, he wanted to kill it."

"But . . ."

"But he was too afraid to anger the gods again."

"Great," Alex sighed.

"You're so sweet, Theseus," Ariadne said. "Pretending you don't know. It's the punishment my father received from Poseidon. For his arrogance."

"Hold still," one of the women said as she fitted a wig on Alex's head.

"Brother or not, I am not going to fight some monster to the death," Alex declared. "Period."

The Princess tried to suppress a gentle smile.

"Tomorrow morning, no one is going to ask for your permission. They're just going to throw you into the labyrinth. I'm just saying that there may be a way to even the contest."

"My death is no contest," Alex said. "Those are two words that don't belong in the same sentence, especially when that sentence applies to me."

"That's not what you said in your big speech, back in Athens. You said your death was of no consequence if you could free Athens from its enslavement."

"*I* said that?" Alex asked. He had no idea what he'd said back in Athens. He didn't know what Theseus had said, either, but he sure was hating his big mouth right now.

"Look, Princess. The kiss was great, fantastic even," Alex said boldly. "But I've never been to Athens. And I'm not Theseus."

Ariadne and the two women stared at Alex. They were confused.

Alex continued. He had opened his mouth and there was no stopping it now. "This is all just a big mistake. My name is Alex Bellows. I have a sister named Cleo. I was born in Omaha, Nebraska, in the United States."

The princess started laughing. "You have a rich sense of humor, Theseus. A wild imagination. I knew you were the right one."

Alex reached under his tunic and unfolded his sketch of his father. "I just came here looking for someone."

Ariadne shook her head. "No, I've never seen him. I'd remember—he would look very out of place in Crete." The other women nodded their agreement. "The Minotaur is a poison that is destroying my home, my life, and my friends. You, Theseus, are the only one who can stop it."

"No way, Princess," Alex disagreed.

Ariadne wouldn't hear of it. "I'm willing to betray my father," she said. "I will betray him to save a kingdom. I just need to know that when it's done, when the Minotaur is dead, you will take me with you."

Alex's eyes nearly jumped from their sockets, and his mouth went slack. "You want to come with me?"

Ariadne nodded, demure and sweet. "Kill the monster. Take me away with you."

Alex swallowed. *Who could resist? So the monster is all-powerful? Who cares? Doesn't love conquer all?* "You got it, Princess. I'm your man." Alex wasn't sure where his bravado suddenly came from, but when he looked at the beautiful eyes and waiting lips of Ariadne, he really didn't care.

Ariadne's feelings for Alex—or were they for Theseus?—were genuine. She smiled and took his hand. "You will be the new champion, Theseus. And I will be yours."

"After meeting you, Princess, I realize that I only go where the gods send me," Alex said. He could hear Cleo laughing on the other side of the plasma screen.

"You have courage, and my love to help you," the princess said, thrilled by Alex's bravery. "Is there anything else you desire?"

Alex thought of the Athenians in the cell below. "I can't abandon my friends, Princess. I can't turn my back on them and leave them behind."

"Courage and love shall save us all," the Princess responded. She pulled him gently by the hand. "Come on. If we can get to Daedalus, he can help you. If nothing else, he knows the labyrinth. He built it."

Wait a minute, Alex thought. *Daedalus? I know this!* "The inventor, right?" he asked, already knowing the answer. "He had a son, uh, Icarus!" He turned to Ariadne.

"Daedalus built wings and Icarus put them on and flew too close to the sun," he said excitedly. "The wings were held together with wax, the heat from the sun melted the wax, and poor

Icarus fell into the sea. That's all she wrote for him!"

Ariadne and the women had no idea what he was talking about.

"The last time I saw him, 'poor' Icarus was very much alive and very much not falling into the sea," Ariadne said. "Shall we see him for ourselves?"

The door to the royal bedchamber opened and one of Princess Ariadne's personal guards stepped in. Alex recognized him as one of the men who had brought him there.

"Princess," the guard said, "the halls are crawling with your father's patrols."

"Let them crawl all they want, they won't find Theseus," the Princess responded proudly. She stepped aside and revealed the newly disguised Alex in his dress and wig.

"Check it out, bud," Alex said. "Does it bring out the color of my eyes?" The women laughed, and even the guard smiled.

"That'll work," the guard said. "And the gods should get a laugh out of it."

Chapter Thirteen

"**This place is** worse than Dr. Frankenstein's laboratory!" Alex declared, greeted by a mountain of chaos and clutter.

"This place" was Daedalus's workshop, or at least what could be seen of it. If there were any tables hidden beneath the vials of fluid, mortars and pestles, bowls, and sketches, Alex certainly couldn't see them. The brown stone walls were covered with astral charts, wind charts, solar charts, lunar charts, maps, and messages.

And in the midst of the visual cacophony

hung a delicate pair of wings, as beautiful as any seen on the back of the gentlest angel.

Ariadne and Alex entered the workshop. Alex stepped over a large spring and a small cauldron of something so foul smelling that he instantly grabbed his nostrils and held his breath.

In the far corner of the workshop sat a bald old man hunched over a small wooden table, working on a second pair of wings. The man heard Alex gag and immediately turned to face his uninvited guests.

"Don't touch anything!" The man's voice was cranky and reminded Alex of his own father after a few sleepless nights.

"Is that Daedalus?" Alex whispered to Ariadne.

"Who else could stand to live like this?" she responded. "Now shush!"

Ariadne made her way to Daedalus, and Alex examined the wings hanging from the ceiling as Icarus entered, carrying a bucket full of freshly plucked feathers.

"I wouldn't fly too high with those if I were you," Alex said, mixing a joke with a warning.

Daedalus rose from his seat faster than Alex would have thought the old man could move. He pushed past Ariadne and quickly stood toe to toe with Alex. The old man had drying wax and feathers stuck to his hands. His face was small and his wrinkled skin wrinkled even more as he squinted at Alex, sizing him up.

"You know something about wings, do you?" Daedalus rocked forward onto his toes to gain every last inch of possible height. "Perhaps you've flown, actually been to the sky yourself? No?"

"Actually . . . yes." Alex had been in an airplane several times and thought very little of the whole process.

"Liar!" Icarus shouted at Alex, suddenly offended at his preposterous claim. "We're the first! And whatever my father builds works! Perfectly!"

Ariadne glared at Alex and stepped between him and Icarus. "Of course the wings will fly. He didn't mean to suggest they wouldn't, did you?"

"Just offering some friendly advice," Alex assured them.

"I'll fly as high as I want!" Icarus boasted, as if the words themselves would beat Alex back.

"That's because you're an idiot," Alex said, smirking.

Ariadne smacked Alex in the hip. Alex found himself at the receiving end of her glare again, but this time she was flushed with anger rather than shock.

"Alex, this may be the only guy in the world who can help you." Cleo's voice chimed in like a nagging conscience.

Alex nodded to both Ariadne and the unseen Cleo.

"Actually, the young lady who needs a shave is quite right," Daedalus said, retreating a few steps from Alex. His attitude shifted from cranky to not so cranky in the blink of an eye. "I worry about my son. Stubborn. Problem with kids is, you give them wings, there's no stopping them."

"The young lady is actually Theseus," Ariadne confessed, not realizing that only a blind man would've fallen for the disguise.

"Of course she is," Daedalus replied, returning to his second set of wings. "Anyone who speaks so loudly of killing the Minotaur would naturally come to me."

"I didn't mean I could do it without your help." Alex did his best to cover. So far his charm hadn't worked very well in ancient Greece. Maybe this was his chance.

"Oh, yes, you did," Daedalus countered, seeing through Alex's ploy. "Even so, I'm going to help you anyway, because I can't stand being stuck on this island anymore."

"I'm grateful. I won't forget this." Ariadne

touched Daedalus's shoulder and smiled at the old man.

"No need," Daedalus quickly began, hiding his embarrassment. "When Theseus kills the beast—*if* he kills the beast—there'll be confusion. A perfect time for Icarus and me to put on our wings and escape."

"I hope the winds are with you," Alex said, surprised at his own sincerity.

Daedalus offered a warm smile. "Spoken like an Athenian prince."

Daedalus waved his hands toward Ariadne's ladies-in-waiting. They reacted quickly, helping Alex remove his womanly disguise.

"This monster is as brutal an enemy as you'll ever face," Daedalus continued, not one to wait for anything or anyone. "I have some tools that might help you."

Daedalus examined Alex, now in his princely Athenian garb.

"An Athenian tunic. Very good. It'll help hide the weapons you need."

As if reading his father's mind, Icarus produced a small, ornately carved ivory box. Daedalus lifted the box before Alex's eyes.

"Perhaps the most important thing you'll need is within this very box," Daedalus boasted.

Alex briefly pondered this riddle and wondered whether he should answer, but he quickly realized that Daedalus preferred hearing himself talk more than listening to anyone else. Alex's silence was broken by the hinges of the creaking box.

"Behold!" Daedalus announced, and reached into the box. "String!"

"String! What am I supposed to do with that? Tie up his pinky finger?" Alex huffed, irritated at the disappointing revelation.

"Daedalus, I expected more than this!" Ariadne added, looking shocked.

"The labyrinth is the most complex maze ever built. What good is killing the beast if you then die of starvation wandering its passages? Hmmm?"

Alex's eyes widened with understanding, and he snatched the string from Daedalus's hand. "Okay. Score one point for you," he said, and hid the string under his tunic.

"Trust the string. It will lead you safely out again."

Once again, Icarus produced the next gem for Daedalus's presentation. It was a plain sword hilt, its blade missing. Alex hoped it was magic or maybe a light saber—he would flick a switch and *Whoosh!* But then Alex realized that myth or no, this was an ancient weapon, not a special effect.

"Remember that things aren't always what they seem," Daedalus commented, handing the granite hilt to Alex.

Alex felt the weight fill his hand. It was surprisingly light, but without a blade, what good would it do him?

"You have to strike the Minotaur while he's sleeping," Daedalus informed Alex. "When he's awake, even your strength is no match for him."

"Awake, asleep, how will this hurt him without a blade?" Alex asked.

"This is just for practice," Daedalus replied. "The weight is exactly right."

"It's light as a feather," Alex commented, slashing and stabbing at the air with the hilt.

"Princess, you have to get back to your quarters before your absence is noticed," Daedalus announced. "There are passages from here that will take Theseus back to the prison. I'll see to it."

Ariadne stepped forward to protest, but Daedalus would have none of it. He waved to the ladies-in-waiting once more, and they moved to Ariadne's side.

She sighed and stepped closer to Alex. He looked into her eyes and smiled, trying to tell

86

her it would be okay. Ariadne fell into his arms, and the two hugged tightly, breaking away only to offer each other a kiss—perhaps their last kiss on this Earth, as Ariadne would not see Alex/ Theseus again before he went to meet his destiny within the labyrinth.

"Time enough for that when you get to Athens," Daedalus said, interrupting the two youths.

"I'll be there when you come out," Ariadne called back to Alex as Daedalus led her to the door.

The moment Ariadne disappeared with her ladies-in-waiting, Daedalus snatched the sword hilt from Alex's hands, then stabbed a gnarled finger in his face.

"Remember this well," Daedalus growled.

"You bet I will," Alex said, staring at the door Ariadne had just walked through.

"Not her! My words!" Daedalus spat, and twisted Alex's ear like a strict teacher who had just caught a napping pupil.

"Remember this well," Daedalus repeated, stressing each word.

"How could I forget?" Alex said sardonically, and rubbed his ear.

"Fifty-five paces into the first passage, find its match," Daedalus said slowly, pacing several steps and holding up the sword hilt to emphasize his words.

"What does that mean?" Alex asked.

"The hilt in the labyrinth is attached to the finest blade ever made," Daedalus explained. "It's there in case our glorious but rash King Minos one day sends me to the Minotaur."

"And you'd give it up for me?" Alex was touched by Daedalus's apparent sacrifice.

"It's not my only secret." Daedalus smiled and patted Alex on the back.

Alex replied with an understanding nod. They exchanged no more words. There was no need. Their admiration for each other's bravery showed in their eyes.

Daedalus led Alex to a bookshelf. He pulled a torch attached to the wall, and the oak shelves creaked to one side, revealing a dimly lit passage.

"May the gods be with you, Theseus," Daedalus said, and nudged Alex into the passage.

Alex took a step and stopped.

"Have you seen this man?" Alex pulled his papyrus drawing from his tunic.

Daedalus shook his head.

Alex hesitated, afraid to ask the next question. "The Minotaur," he began. "Have you ever seen him?"

"Only in my darkest nightmares, my son. Only in my darkest nightmares."

Chapter Fourteen

"**What are you** supposed to do with this?" Philitas asked.

Alex snatched the ball of string from Philitas's hand.

"It's all very complicated science stuff," Alex said. "I don't expect you to understand."

"Why don't you use it to find your way back out?" Leto asked, taking the ball from Alex.

"Yeah. I'll think about that one," Alex replied.

"You seem a little tense," Kadilus pointed out. "Are your spirits low?"

"Just chilling."

"I could get you a blanket."

"No. I mean . . ." Alex realized that modern slang was meaningless here. "I mean I'm fine."

"You're not scared, are you?" Kadilus pressed.

"Scared!" Alex gasped, trying his best to hide the fact that he was scared.

"Of course not," Kadilus said. "Nothing to be afraid of, if it's true that there'll be a sword there for you. Too bad it's not the sword that does the slaying, but the man who carries it."

Alex was really beginning to dislike Kadilus. "What's your point?" he grumbled.

"Just don't doubt yourself. You know how dangerous doubt can be."

Alex leered at Kadilus. Unhappy with the direction of the conversation, Alex stormed over to the rest of the group.

"Gimme that!" Alex spat, and grabbed the string from Leto. "It's not a toy!"

A murmur of shock vibrated through the group as Alex stomped to the far side of the cell.

"There's a way out."

Kadilus was at it again.

"What do you mean?" Alex asked.

"I mean we can escape." Kadilus's voice dropped to a whisper.

"How do we sneak ten people out of a dungeon?"

"We don't. It would just be you and me, Theseus."

Alex moved past beginning to dislike Kadilus to definitely disliking Kadilus. Before Alex could respond, Kadilus continued.

"They're going to die anyway. You don't really think you're going to kill the Minotaur, do you?"

"You think I'm going to sneak off and abandon everybody? What kind of an Athenian are you?" Alex chastised him.

"What makes you think I'm an Athenian at all?" Kadilus's words hissed through his teeth as he smiled at Alex.

"Who are you?" Alex's sharp question was answered by Kadilus's sharp silence. Alex took a step away from Kadilus, as if the stench of his proximity were too much for Alex to bear.

Alex returned to Leto and the others, casting a final glance back at Kadilus. The others, unaware of Kadilus's plotted betrayal, embraced their hero with pats on the back and enthusiastic well-wishing.

"Time to say goodbye to your friends, Theseus."

Alex turned. Standing in the door was King Minos himself, two armed soldiers at his side. A smile lifted Minos's fat cheeks.

"Say goodbye to your friends," Minos repeated, "and hello to your gods."

Chapter Fifteen

The double doors stood before Alex like a great barrier between known and unknown, life and death. Their mammoth wood beams stood twelve feet high and could withstand the battering of a crazed elephant. A huge timber bolt slid across the double doors to prevent any movement. Massive hinges resisted force, weather, and aging.

In a word, the doors were impregnable.

Four soldiers moved to the wooden bolt and slid it open with great effort. Behind Alex, two drums beat in alternating rhythms as the same men grabbed the enormous brass handles on each door and struggled to gain footing in the sand. Once, twice, thrice, and the hinges creaked and reluctantly gave in to the defeat of movement.

Alex turned to Ariadne in the royal box. "The presence of one so beautiful honors my victory today, Princess," he boasted, then turned away from the glowing Ariadne and the seething King Minos. "I am so dead," Alex sighed under his breath.

He took one final look around the arena. The seats were packed with eager Cretans, hungry for one more day of spectacle. But this time, things were different. There were no dancers, no priests, no men in bull heads, no cheers.

There were only Alex and the labyrinth.

King Minos made a silent gesture to one of the soldiers. He moved toward Alex with his sword.

"Chill out, man," Alex said, and headed into the labyrinth of his own volition.

Alex looked back one final time into the tearful eyes of Ariadne and then plunged headlong into darkness.

The thunder of wood slamming against wood jolted through his body and rattled his teeth.

"I'm scared," Cleo's voice whispered in his head.

"Nothing to be scared about," Alex lied to his sister.

Before him lay a system of passageways that looked messier than a plateful of twisting spaghetti.

"Try Daedalus's string," Cleo suggested.

Alex removed the ball from under his tunic and tied one end to one of the wooden doors. He dropped the ball to the floor. Like a cat chasing a mouse, the ball shot off into the darkness, rolling away under its own power in a crazed fury.

"Wow!" Alex gasped, shocked at the magical properties of the gift. "Did you see that?"

"Shhh!" Cleo's voiced warned in his head. "You don't want to wake up the Minotaur."

Alex looked at his feet and saw that not only would the string find its own way to the Minotaur, but it also glowed a soft fluorescent blue to guide its user. Like a giant arrow pointing "this way," the blue line ignored false passages and dead ends and rolled directly to the heart of the matter—the Minotaur's lair.

Alex took a deep breath and made a silent wish, then paced off four steps exactly as Daedalus had shown him. After the fourth pace, Alex inspected the wall. In the dim light of the glowing thread, he could see nothing but stone. He felt blindly in the shadows, hoping the sword would be as wonderful as the once-mocked ball of string.

"Be there . . . ," he whispered.

His fingers rubbed against the coarse surface of the wall, his soft pink skin scuffed by the abrasive rock. Nothing. Alex clenched his teeth. *Daedalus said it would be here. It has to be!*

Suddenly Alex felt a curve with his thumb. His twitching fingers instantly clenched the man-made shape like a tired swimmer clinging to a life preserver.

Alex gave a slight tug and the sword, perfectly matched in color to blend with the wall, broke away from the rocky surface.

Alex was by no means an expert with swords, but in the faintly lit cavern, even his untrained eye could see the beauty and craftsmanship of Daedalus's creation, with its gray blade and matching hilt. Alex caressed the weapon with a delicate care that belied its intended use.

Alex sliced at the air and stabbed at an invisible target. A warmth filled his muscles, and for the first time he felt the seeds of hope take root. He took a deep breath, checked the glowing string, and moved forward.

One lucky blow, just one, Alex thought as he frantically practiced.

Alex was immediately thankful for his blue guide. Save for an occasional lone torch casting a dim glow, each passage looked the same, every gray wall blurring into the next. A stink like rotting fruit at the bottom of a garbage heap hung in the air and filled Alex's lungs. Cobwebs grabbed him at every turn, making him feel more like a fly than a spider—more like prey than predator.

"What am I doing here?" he asked Cleo. "I'm just some stupid kid who can't even pass algebra."

"Do your best, Alex" was all she said.

"My best? You make it sound like I'm playing basketball! And now that I think about it, that's what I should be doing, not wandering around this rotten place looking for a nightmare."

"I know, Alex."

"Yeah, yeah. This whole thing just ticks me off a little. What does any of this have to do with finding Dad?"

Cleo didn't answer.

Alex ignored the smell and the cobwebs and pressed forward into the darkness. He picked up his pace, not eager to meet the Minotaur but eager to end the anxiety, eager to end the chase.

He stumbled. The shock of touching something in the dark, on the smooth dirt floor, made him retreat several steps into the light of a nearby torch.

He collected his thoughts and pulled the torch from its sconce. He held it in front of him and looked to see what he had kicked.

Immediately he regretted his decision.

"This is getting real freaky."

Before him lay a man—or what was left of a man. Decomposed flesh clung to mangled bones. The smell made Alex gag, and he could no longer suppress his fear. The pageant, the fight, Daedalus, Ariadne, it had all seemed like an amazing dream. Everything shattered, and the reality of death hit Alex like a fierce slap in the face.

"Oh my gosh, Alex . . ." He heard Cleo's voice trail off in his head.

"Yeah. Yeah" was all he could say.

Alex raised the torch. He was about to move on when a glittering reflection caught his eye. It was near the hand of the skeleton, and as loath as Alex was to take something from the peaceful rest of death, he thought it might help him in avenging this and so many other needless deaths.

As well as prevent his own.

Alex had never met Acheon, but he now stood over the only evidence that the young warrior had ever existed. "Sorry," Alex whispered, and scooped the item from the sand. It was a star-shaped amulet, a green jewel at its heart. Perhaps a gift, perhaps something the man had held on to in his final moments to give him peace, to remember love. In either case, the only person the star amulet would ever help was lying at Alex's feet, a heap of bones.

Alex wasn't alone. As he dropped the star amulet back into the skeleton's hand, he heard a low, heavy breathing behind him. Alex moved slowly, carefully, as if he were sneaking up on a fly cleaning its wings on the windowsill in his bedroom. His palm, moist with sweat, tightened on the hilt of his sword.

Alex squinted, hoping to catch a glimpse in his peripheral vision of what waited behind him. A shadow pressed flat against the wall, and Alex was certain this would be his final moment.

Alex bit his lip and spun, sword drawn back with fury and fear, adrenaline pumping through his veins like water surging through a fire hose.

"Kadilus!" Alex shouted, stunned that the deadly creature was in fact his Athenian comrade.

"You look so very surprised," Kadilus said with amusement. "I love that."

"Shhh!" Alex warned, ignoring Kadilus's comment. Alex looked around for a moment to make sure they were alone, then added, "What are you doing here? How did you get here?"

Kadilus was calm, and Alex swore he noted a change in his demeanor. It was as if Alex was seeing the true Kadilus now, the one who had tipped his hand when he tempted Alex to leave his friends to die alone. Kadilus strolled up to Alex, dropping a passing glance on the unfortunate soul who had fallen victim to the Minotaur.

"I'm here to plead for the Minotaur's life," Kadilus said, placing an arm around Alex like an old chum.

"Are you getting this?" Alex heard Cleo ask.

"I'm here to beg you to walk away and let him be," Kadilus finished.

Alex wasn't exactly sure what was happening. Why would Kadilus ask for such a thing? But then, this wasn't the first odd request Kadilus had made of him.

"Too late for that," Alex said coldly, and shrugged off Kadilus's embracing arm.

Alex redoubled his resolve and headed down the passage, leaving Kadilus to his own fate—or so Alex thought. That was when Alex heard it and stopped dead in his tracks. It wasn't the monstrous howl of the Minotaur. No, it was two words from Kadilus.

"Alex, Alex," he said.

Chapter Sixteen

"How do you know my name?" Alex yelled at Kadilus.

"The Minotaur is no vicious monster." Kadilus had no interest in pausing to answer Alex's question. He had a point to make, and neither Alex's confusion nor his anger would distract him from his objective. "He's just another one of the pathetic screwups by the gods. They mess with people and the next thing you know, you've got some pitiful creature living its life in agony, and then you just tuck it away and call it a story."

Despite Kadilus's claim that he was pleading for the life of the Minotaur, his tone was as cold and unemotional as it had been when he had cast doubt on Alex back in the prisoners' pen. It was almost as if Kadilus didn't really care whether the Minotaur lived or died—he only wanted to stop Alex.

"Yeah, a pitiful creature that kills everything that comes in its way," Alex sneered. "Now forget the Minotaur and tell me how you know my real name."

Once more, Alex's question fell on deaf ears.

"Nonsense! The Minotaur doesn't kill everything that comes into the labyrinth. He hides! He is so ashamed of what he looks like, he hides. Almost everyone who died in here starved to death before they ever found him. This is all a joke, really. Nothing but a tremendous joke played on all of us by the gods and King Minos, and you, dear Alex, are the punch line."

"Who are you!" Alex screamed, the words exploding from his lungs at Kadilus's mocking tone.

"I'm just about anybody, Alex. Sometimes all at the same time." Kadilus hid a chuckle at the cleverness of his own words. "And if you won't leave . . ."

Where a moment before there had been an empty hand, Kadilus now revealed that he carried a sword identical to Alex's. Kadilus bared the sword and waited a moment, as if to silently offer Alex one final chance to change his mind. Alex raised the tip of his own sword and clenched the handle.

Kadilus charged.

Every muscle in Alex's body tightened. Kadilus let out a small shout, and Alex prepared to parry.

"Look out! Look out!" he heard Cleo yell in his head.

"Shhh! I need to concentrate!" Alex stabbed back as Kadilus's sword swung down on him.

Alex dove to the right, and Kadilus's sword slashed into the ground.

Before Alex could regain his senses, Kadilus charged for another strike. Alex raised his sword at the last instant. The blades clanged together with a surprisingly dull crack. Kadilus drew his sword back and swung down on Alex's again and again, driving Alex back a step with each blow.

"Hit him back! Hit him!" Cleo shouted in his head.

"I know!" Alex yelled back, panicked.

Kadilus raised his sword, and Alex saw his opening. Alex stabbed at Kadilus and missed, but the attack worked to create some space between the two opponents.

"Why are you doing this?" Alex asked with gasping breaths.

Kadilus considered the question for a moment, then replied, "Do you see, if I stop you from killing the Minotaur, there will never be a story about Theseus and the Minotaur."

"So?" Alex said, puffing.

"So I will kill a small piece of culture, and a small piece of mankind will die with it. If I were to destroy all the myths, what would mankind have to believe in? Nothing! Without your culture, without your myths, you humans will be lost, without direction. Chaos will fall upon civilization, and I will rise up and take control of all you sheep. I will rule!"

"You're insane."

Even before the final word passed Alex's lips, Kadilus was on top of him again, this time aiming a sweeping blow at Alex's torso. Alex inverted his hand and thrust his sword downward, deflecting Kadilus's advance. Alex quickly slid his own blade up the length of Kadilus's, past the hilt, and swept directly into Kadilus's midsection.

The sword passed through Kadilus as if he were a ghost.

"Tricky, no?" Kadilus laughed.

Alex dropped the sword to his side, and his mouth fell open. *How can I ever win this fight?* he wondered.

"There's that surprised look again. Watching you with that sword, I'd say the beast probably has nothing to fear from you after all."

Kadilus filled his chest with the stale air of the labyrinth. He tilted his head back, and a sharp, haunting shriek like the howling of a thousand crippled cats rose from his lungs.

Alex covered his ears, and back in the study, Cleo did the same.

"This can't be good," Alex whispered to his sister.

His remark was prophetic. A deeper roar overwhelmed and killed the final faint echoes of Kadilus's own foul scream.

"Seems I woke the baby," Kadilus joyfully

pointed out as a second roar issued forth from the unseen Minotaur.

"I'm not done with you!" Alex yelled at Kadilus.

There was another roar, the distant stomping of feet.

"Oh, I think you are," Kadilus smugly replied.

Like a storm drawing closer with each shattering burst of thunder, Alex could hear the Minotaur's roar growing louder, the pounding footsteps closing the distance between them.

"Chow time," Kadilus said, and perched on a rock to watch the show.

"Be careful, Alex." Cleo's voice was tense. She did her best to cover the fear, but Alex knew that he was more frightened than she was.

Alex faced the direction the footsteps came from. The sword suddenly felt heavier than a lead block. His fingers twitched under its burden. Sweat ran down the back of his neck and soaked into his tunic. Alex thought he saw two coals burning red in the darkness of the narrow passage before him.

Okay, you can do this, Alex calmly reminded

himself. *It's no more difficult than asking out a girl—a popular, pretty girl who hates you.*

The sound of the footsteps was joined by a jarring snort.

Alex swallowed. Nothing could have prepared him for what moved forward from the darkness.

"Oh my—"

The Minotaur stood ten feet tall, with the body of a man and the head of a bull. Had the labyrinth been opened to the sky, surely the beast's massive head would have blocked out the sun like an ominous sign of impending doom. Its coarse, matted black hair jutted from the sides of its head. Its mouth was lined with rotting teeth, eager to bite Alex in two. Snot ran from its nose like a leaking faucet, and a thick glob of drool dangled off its raw, cracked lips. Bloodshot eyes, dead of all emotion save hate, glared at Alex. The putrid stench of the unholy stung Alex's senses.

"Have fun," Kadilus quipped.

Alex's throat dried like a rotten prune and he swallowed hard against his fear. A sword was supposed to stop this . . . this . . . thing? *A tank would be more like it,* he thought.

Alex raised the sword. He'd seen tons of

sword fights in the movies. Mustering every last ounce of courage, he dug in and prepared to deliver a blow.

Just like Luke Skywalker would do it, he told himself.

The beast roared, and the walls shuddered. Alex blinked, and the next instant the Minotaur was on top of him. It swung a muscular arm, and Alex flew across the passage. The sword clanged from his sweaty grip as he thudded to the ground.

"He's too fast!" Alex cried out.

The beast lowered its head to charge, horns first. Alex scrambled to his feet. He grabbed the Minotaur's horns and leapfrogged the length of the creature's body to temporary safety, but not without injury. His arm caught on the left horn. Pain shot through his arm to the shoulder. But he had no time to worry about blood or pain. As long as he could stand, as long as he could see, he could fight.

Alex dove for the sword.

The Minotaur lifted a huge rock and threw it at Alex as if it were a loaf of bread. Alex dodged aside, and the rock smashed against the wall behind him.

"I need a gun! This is crazy!" Alex yelled out to Cleo.

Long past the concerns of a fair fight, Alex grabbed a handful of dirt from the labyrinth floor and flung it into the golf ball–sized eyes of the Minotaur. The beast wailed, and Alex charged.

"Did I mention that Matt Bellows called me Gorgos?" Kadilus yelled out from his rock.

Alex stopped dead in his tracks and spun to face the man he had known as Kadilus.

"My father?" Alex yelled.

"Alex! He knows about Dad!" Alex could hear Cleo shouting in his head.

Instead of finding a possible answer to the riddle of his father's whereabouts, Alex only saw an empty rock. Kadilus . . . Gorgos . . . had disappeared.

But the Minotaur had not.

His eyes cleared of the stinging dirt, the beast roared and charged Alex. Gorgos's distraction had worked, and now the Minotaur seethed with anger.

Alex did the only thing he could think of. He ran.

"I've gotta find a way out, Cleo. I can't beat that thing! I can barely use a sword!"

"If I see anything on the plasma screen, I'll tell you!" Cleo assured him.

Alex raced down one passage, then another, then a third. He finally stopped at a four-way intersection, his lungs gasping for air, his muscles begging for rest. His respite was fleeting, as he immediately heard the stomping feet of the Minotaur closing ground.

"Damn it! I don't know where I am! Can you see the string anywhere?"

"No."

"I gotta think. I gotta think," Alex puffed. "I fought Ken Meyers once in tenth grade. Yeah. He was huge. I stood up to him!"

"What happened?"

"He beat the snot outta me."

Alex considered each possible direction, then fled down the darkest passageway. A moment later, the Minotaur arrived at the intersection. It stopped and sniffed the wall and the stagnant air, then urgently raced off in the same direction as Alex.

Alex continued down the passage and bolted through the T-intersection. He came to a skidding halt and raced back to the T. Something had caught his eye.

"There!" he yelled to Cleo. "Light!"

It was a dim light, but it was light. And light meant the sky and a way out of the labyrinth! A huge sigh of relief exploded from Alex's lungs and he raced toward his shimmering salvation.

Chapter Seventeen

Alex felt giddy and couldn't hold back his laughter as he ran to the light. He no longer heard the pounding steps of the Minotaur. Nothing would stop him from finding freedom—or from finding out exactly what Gorgos knew about his father.

"Cleo, when I am out of here, the first thing I'm going to do is find King Minos and pop him right in the—"

Alex reached the end of the passage and stopped dead in his tracks. A twisting agony wrenched through his stomach, and he wasn't sure whether he should swear or cry.

"No . . . no . . ."

He stood in the lair of the Minotaur. The sky . . . the light . . . was actually a dozen torches that lined the walls, casting an orangish yellow hue across the large room.

Alex scanned the lair. A pile of straw substituted for a bed in the corner. A tub collected water that dripped from a slime-covered crack in the wall. The home of the Minotaur was as pathetic as its monstrous appearance. But before an ounce of sympathy could seep from Alex's heart, he saw the remains, the horrible remains of the innocent victims who had been cast into the labyrinth before him.

A thousand thoughts raced through Alex's mind. Faces of friends flashed in his head. These young bodies could be Philthy or Mike or Cleo. They could all have been Alex's friends, and maybe some of them had been Theseus's friends.

Back home, Alex's biggest worries were homework and school. He never had to worry about being a sacrifice to a murderous Minotaur. Now all those problems seemed so small to Alex, so insignificant compared to the fate of the Athenians forced into the labyrinth.

Young men and women, probably no older than Alex, whose only crime was that they didn't have the strength or the means to fight the monster who hunted them down the blind passages of the labyrinth. In their misery, their suffering, their sacrifice, Alex found courage. Seeing their rotting remains sickened Alex to the depth of his soul, but for the first time, he completely understood why Theseus had volunteered to face the Minotaur. Whether it was the bravery of Theseus or his own resolve taking root, Alex felt strength return to his aching limbs.

"No more," he said aloud, just as Theseus had said so many weeks before. "No one will ever have to die here again."

The words surprised Alex, but not the courage. Certainly he had spent most of his life dodging and charming his way out of trouble, but there was no dodge or charm here. This was wrong, what was done to these young Athenians. It was wrong, and Alex was the only one who could stop it.

Alex wiped the sweat from his brow and tightened his grip. He heard a dull snorting behind him, followed by a low growl, a cruel growl from the pit of the beast's hungry stomach.

"Come on," Alex muttered through gritted teeth. "Let's see what you've got, you big ugly pile of puke."

Alex didn't turn. He didn't move. Fear pounded against his spirit, trying to finally break him, but Alex refused to let go of the courage he had just sparked in his heart.

The beast leaped. Alex heard it roar. Alex spun and dropped to the floor like a falling tree. The beast, eagerly anticipating the end of the hunt, sailed through the air to pounce on him.

The last thing the Minotaur saw was Alex raising his sword in a flash to meet its body. The Minotaur's great red eyes widened, but it was too late. It was in midleap. There was nothing it could do but land—land on Alex, land on his sword, land on its doom.

The beast crashed down on Alex, and the sword plunged through its heart and killed it instantly. Dead limbs collapsed on Alex, and the full weight of the massive body threatened to crush him. Alex gathered the last of his strength and tilted the sword.

The Minotaur, sword buried in its chest up

to the hilt, plopped to the side, and Alex gasped a deep breath of life.

The labyrinth was silent. Empty. Dead. But Alex was alive and had fulfilled both Theseus's and his own promise: No one would ever die in the labyrinth again.

"Alex . . . I . . . I just want you to know . . . I wanted to tell you . . . ," Cleo stammered in his head.

"I know, sis. I know."

"So now what? How are you going to get out of there?"

Alex looked around the room. He smiled. In the corner, he finally noticed a thin, delicate, glowing blue line . . . the exact kind one would see once a ball of magical string had completely unwound itself.

Chapter Eighteen

The sun beat down from the Cretan sky. Leto looked up at the blue sky and the billowing clouds and thanked the gods she had lived to see such a glorious day.

And may I live to see another, she silently prayed.

No one had really questioned the disappearance of Kadilus. Once the guards had discovered his absence, they merely told King Minos that Kadilus had died of fright and that they, the guards, had disposed of the body. They feared that if they told the king Kadilus was gone, they would be sent to the Minotaur in his stead.

The Athenians believed he had escaped, given freedom as a blessing from the gods.

No one suspected that he was really Gorgos in disguise.

Now Leto, Philitas, and the other Athenians were huddled before the large doors, guarding the entrance to the labyrinth. Alex had entered nearly an hour before, and soon it would be their turn to meet their end at the hands of the beast within.

They huddled together like a flock of skittish sheep. Leto and Philitas did their best to assure the other Athenians that Theseus would save them, but in their hearts, even they doubted that their hero had defeated the Minotaur.

"If we cannot face the Minotaur as its killers, then we shall at least meet it as the brave men and women of Athens," Leto said. "Let us show Crete of what stuff we are made."

A brave boast indeed, and as Philitas faced the giant wooden doors that stood between him and his death, he prayed as he had never done before that the gods' mercy would spare them as it had done Kadilus. A soldier jabbed at Philitas, and in the soreness of his ribs he thought he had the gods' answer to his plea.

"Next time I'm praying to the Egyptian gods!" Philitas called to the heavens.

The crowd played its part in the grand tragedy as well. They jeered and shouted at the Athenians, determined to deprive them of dignity even in their last moments alive.

As they had done earlier with Alex, the soldiers began the ritual of opening the massive doors to the labyrinth. The hinges gave way and the doors creaked open, but as daylight cut into the darkness of the labyrinth, the creaking of the doors was drowned out by the screams of horror and shock that issued from the Cretans in the arena.

From the gloom of the labyrinth did not come the roar of the Minotaur that they had become so accustomed to hearing. Instead, from the darkness rolled the head of the Minotaur.

Alex stepped out of the labyrinth and into the nourishing rays of the sun that hung in the western sky. He had been in the labyrinth for an hour at most, but he bathed in the sun's warmth with all the welcoming love of a man who had spent six months in a cave.

Alex was bruised. Blood still ran from his arm, and dried blood clung to his nose and lip.

He felt as if he had just finished football practice—without wearing pads. As the adrenaline finally stopped pumping through his veins, he collapsed into the arms of Leto.

Philitas and the other Athenians quickly gathered around Leto and Alex. They hugged Alex, cheered him, congratulated him, and finally hoisted him upon their shoulders and paraded him around the arena. Alex raised his hands above his head in a gesture of triumph.

At first the Cretan crowd was shocked into silence, but soon they too cheered their new hero, they too rose to their feet and clamored uproariously at Alex's victory over the monster.

"This must be what it's like to win the Super Bowl," Alex suggested to Leto, who had no clue about what he was referring to.

In her royal box, Ariadne nearly collapsed. Tears poured down her cheeks like waterfalls. Her Theseus had returned. Her love had come back to her.

All in the arena celebrated except for one. King Minos gritted his teeth and glared at Alex. Alex immediately caught his angry stare and threw Minos a giant thumbs-up. Minos didn't understand what the foreign gesture meant, but he knew he loathed it nonetheless. He snatched his scepter from a servant's hand and stormed from the royal box.

Philitas lifted the huge Minotaur's head. "This goes on the wall of my den!"

Alex strolled proudly to the ring's center. He had won, but somehow it didn't feel right yet. *What would Theseus do now?* he wondered.

Alex thrust the bloody sword above his head and instantly killed the tumultuous cheers of the crowd. He scanned their silent faces.

"You cheer for death?" he yelled out. "Would you have cheered for my death? King Minos's? Your brothers'? Your own?" Alex paused. A murmur ran through the crowd. "You are fools! It was your savage hunger that allowed so many to die in the Minotaur's lair! The Athenians are your brothers as you are ours. Let us go forward together from this day, not cheering death but celebrating life!"

The crowd exploded into thunderous cheering.

"Wow, Alex," Cleo whispered. "Where did that come from?"

"Beats me," Alex said, basking in the roaring applause, "but it sure felt good."

• • •

Once the festivities waned, Leto, Philitas, and the other Athenians left Alex and Ariadne behind to prepare for their triumphant morning departure back to Athens.

Left alone in the now vacant arena, Alex finally felt the wonder of what he had accomplished. But he had no time to bask in glory. He had to find his father.

"We can't wait," he told Ariadne as she bandaged his arm. "By tomorrow your father may change his mind about our leaving. Are you ready?"

Ariadne's only reply was to throw her arms around him.

Unnoticed by either Alex or Ariadne, a mysterious figure watched them from the arena below. His clothes were torn in some places, his features tired and ragged. For a moment, he struggled to gather himself, unsure where he was or how he had gotten there, but the young man standing in the royal box looked so familiar, so comforting. The ragged man collected his thoughts, focused.

"Oh my god!" the ragged man yelled, finally coming to his senses. "Alex! Alex!" he cried out in an even louder voice.

"Sorry, Dr. Bellows," Gorgos said, materializing next to the ragged man. "You're invisible to him."

Dr. Bellows rotated on his right foot and stood face to face with Gorgos, who was still in the form of Kadilus.

"How do you know . . . It's you, isn't it, Gorgos?" Dr. Bellows said, unable to hide the disgust in his voice.

"I thought you might be happier to see me," Gorgos said sarcastically. "Scholar to scholar, so to speak."

"Where am I?" Dr. Bellows was in no mood for games.

"Well, certainly not in your cozy little home." Gorgos topped off this line with a two-step shuffle. All he needed was a rim shot to accompany the wilted punch line. Dr. Bellows was not amused.

"Sorry," Gorgos began, collecting himself. "I thought a little touch of humor might be appreciated at a time like this."

"What do you want?" Dr. Bellows asked coldly.

"My stone." Gorgos abandoned his joking tone and quickly became sullen. "It holds my fate, Dr. Bellows. Maybe my end."

"What do you mean?"

"You saw the arrow," Gorgos said, seething. "It can destroy me! All my efforts are meaningless until the stone is safely back with me! I want my stone!"

For the first time, Gorgos showed emotion beyond cruelty. Dr. Bellows saw desperation in his eyes. It was a look Dr. Bellows could get to like.

"Why are you doing this to me?" Dr. Bellows asked.

Gorgos smiled. "I don't know how you came to be trapped in this world with me, but if I suffer, you shall suffer too. Tell me what you did with my stone. I know you made it disappear!"

"I'd rather be lost here forever than help you get your hands on it," Dr. Bellows defiantly countered, not wanting to admit that he really had no idea what had happened to the Gorgos Stone.

Gorgos calmed himself. He was angry with himself for allowing his emotion to betray so much. He chuckled, rubbed his chin, then said, "Oh, Dr. Bellows, you have no idea how long forever gets to be." Gorgos smiled and nodded in Alex's direction. "Especially for a kid."

"That *is* him!" Dr. Bellows exploded. "I knew it!"

"Everyone thinks it's Theseus, but it is Alex, for the moment. It won't be for much longer."

"Alex! Alex!" Dr. Bellows cried as he raced toward his son.

Alex didn't respond. He never looked away from Ariadne, never blinked an eye.

"Alex!" Dr. Bellows cried out in near agony.

"I don't lie," Gorgos said, appearing between Alex and Dr. Bellows. "He can't hear you, can't see you."

"Alex!"

In the royal box, Alex paused. He tilted his head as if hearing the distant buzzing of a fly. A sense of the familiar drifted through him, almost as if he were experiencing déjà vu. He shook off the sensation, then noticed Ariadne holding up a pendant to hang around his neck.

"That's incredible. It's Dionysus! That's the thing I touched on the plasma screen," Alex said, pointing to the figure molded to the center of the golden pendant.

"To protect us on our journey," Ariadne explained. "The waters of the sea are—"

If Ariadne finished her sentence, Alex never heard her. One moment he was reaching out for

Dionysus, the next he touched the figure, and the next everything went black.

Dr. Bellows noticed a golden, almost invisible shimmer surrounding the body of his son; then Alex disappeared, replaced by the real Theseus.

"Sweet Ariadne," Theseus said as if Alex had never even existed. "I am tired. I feel . . . I feel as if I've just completed an amazing journey."

Dr. Bellows watched Theseus put his arm around Ariadne. The two left the royal box, neither one the wiser that his son had walked in Theseus's stead.

"Alex . . . ," Dr. Bellows moaned. He fell to his knees and fought a pounding desire to cry.

Cleo watched the plasma screen. She never saw her father in the arena, never saw Gorgos laugh at Dr. Bellows's despair, but she did see Theseus replace Alex. The moment the golden shimmer faded, Cleo instinctively looked around the study for her missing brother.

And he appeared, smack in the room's center.

"You're back! You're back," she yelled, and quickly wheeled to his side.

"Stop kissing me!" Alex flailed his hands in the air in a desperate attempt to avoid his sister's thankful affection.

Cleo rolled back a few feet and caught her breath. "Was Dad there?" she asked.

"I didn't see any sign of him. Nothing."

"Should we tell Mom what happened?" Cleo asked.

"Not until we have some idea what's going on. She'd never let us go back."

"Back . . ." Cleo had known it was coming, but finally hearing it left her shaking.

"Back. Until we find Dad, we can't give up."

Chapter Nineteen

The final bell of the school day had rung only minutes before, but the army of students that had flooded into the hall had just as quickly disappeared through the front doors to freedom. Alex walked beside Cleo. On her lap was a stack of mythology books.

"You, or Theseus, broke Ariadne's heart," Cleo reported, tapping the cover of the uppermost book in her stack. "She was promised to Dionysus, and under threat from the gods, you—Theseus—gave her up."

"Wow. She married a god." Alex didn't consider that such a bad option.

"That makes you happy?"

"Well . . . you know . . . you can't really get jealous about a god!" Alex defended himself. "What about Gorgos? Did you find anything?"

"Nothing. He's not mentioned anywhere. Not a word."

"And Theseus, did he get home?"

"Yes. But . . ." Cleo paused. She held up the book to Alex. "Maybe you should just read it for yourself."

"That bad?" Alex stopped at his locker and spun the dial on the lock.

"Well, after he lost Ariadne, they sailed home under a black sail, and when King Aegeus saw it, he thought it meant his beloved son, Theseus, was dead. He was so overcome with grief, he threw himself into the sea."

Alex stopped working the lock and turned to his sister. "He died?" he gasped.

"For his son. Apparently that's why they call it the Aegean Sea."

Alex absorbed all the information Cleo had dumped on him. His face turned pale as he considered his conclusions.

"You're telling me Theseus killed his father?" Alex reluctantly began.

"It was a mistake, but if you want to look at it that way, yeah, I guess."

There was silence between the two siblings. Alex struggled with his next question, not sure how to phrase it and even more unsure whether he wanted it answered.

"Cleo, if I were Theseus, and Theseus killed his father . . ." Alex paused. This was more difficult than fighting the Minotaur. "Does that mean . . . I killed our dad? I mean, you know, by mistake?"

"I don't think so," Cleo responded. "But there's something I've been scared about too. What if I killed Dad the day I turned off the computer? What if that killed him?"

Before Alex could offer his sister words of reassurance, a shout echoed down the empty school hall.

"Run, Alex! Run!"

It was Philip. Alex raised his hand to say hello to his friend, but Philip bolted past. He skidded to a stop in a T-intersection, quickly considered his options, then rocketed to the left.

Alex and Cleo exchanged a look; then Alex

turned to see what Philip had been escaping from.

"Hello, Bellows. Your friend is pretty fast." Mr. Watt slapped five stapled sheets of paper into Alex's hand. Alex returned a confused look.

"Your makeup exam?" Mr. Watt said.

Cleo always knew when it was time to go, and it was definitely time to go. She held back a laugh and rolled herself down the hall, leaving Alex to his educational fate.

"Oh," Alex sighed, weighing the paper stack in his hand. "Ah, you see . . . last night I, I . . ."

"Last night you were . . ."

"Busy?"

"Busy." Mr. Watt didn't look at all surprised. Alex always had an excuse. Mr. Watt put his hands on his hips. "Something more important than the exam, I'm sure. What? Trolling for girls? Surfing the Net? Saving the world, maybe?"

"Well, slaying the Minotaur, as a matter of fact," Alex replied, trying to hide his smile.

"Good." Alex could've said "flying to the moon" and Mr. Watt would have ignored him with equal ease. "There's not enough of that these days."

Alex put on a sheepish smile and nodded to Mr. Watt.

"And there's not enough of this, either." Mr. Watt did a little finger drum on the test lying in Alex's hand, then pointed him to an empty classroom.

With his eyes Alex followed Mr. Watt's arm, which extended above his head like a signpost. Alex hung his head and drearily marched into the classroom.

Mr. Watt followed close behind. He grabbed the doorknob as he passed and pulled on the thick door. The hinges moaned in protest but ultimately gave in to Mr. Watt's will. The door swung closed. Its slam echoed throughout the deserted halls with a finality that reminded all who could hear of the inevitable doom that would devour Alex.

Or maybe it was just a history test.

Theseus and the Minotaur

The gods of Greek mythology were very jealous and quick to anger. When Poseidon, the god of the sea, demanded the sacrifice of a beautiful white bull to honor him, King Minos of Crete was happy to comply. But the wife of Minos, Queen Pasiphae, loved the bull and would not permit her husband to kill it. So Poseidon punished the king for his disobedience by causing the queen to give birth to the Minotaur, a monstrous creature, half-bull, half-human, who would eat only human flesh.

King Minos employed a brilliant inventor named Daedalus to create a complex maze beneath the castle where they could lock the creature away. The maze was so confusing that only Daedalus, who created it, and the Minotaur, who could see in the dark, knew its every turn. When the Minotaur was hungry, his cries could shake the palace. Finding food for the Minotaur was very hard. For many years, King Minos had to wage war and take prisoners to feed his terrifying son.

Then one of Minos's sons visited Athens, where he was accidentally killed. King Minos told King Aegeus of Athens that unless seven young Athenian men and seven young Athenian women were sent to Crete every nine years as a sacrifice to the Minotaur, he would destroy their city in revenge. King Aegeus agreed to the terms, and the people of Athens unhappily complied.

The third time Athens was forced to send its young men and women, Theseus, the son of Aegeus, volunteered to go. Theseus was a mighty hero who wanted to end the suffering of his people. The old king begged his son not to go, but Theseus would not be dissuaded. He promised his father that when the ship returned from Crete, if its sails were white, he was alive and had killed the monster. If the sails were black, it would mean that Theseus was dead and Athens must still pay with the blood of its people.

When he arrived at Crete, handsome Theseus captured the heart of Ariadne, daughter of King Minos. Ariadne could not allow her new love to die, so she went to Daedalus for advice. Daedalus told her that the Minotaur slept at midnight for one hour. Then and only then could a human hope to slay him. Daedalus gave Ariadne a ball of magic thread that would lead Theseus to the center of the labyrinth and guide him out once his task was done.

Ariadne offered to save Theseus if he would take her with him when he left, and he agreed. She revealed her secrets and led him to the labyrinth's entrance. He followed the thread around winding hallways and past the bones of other victims, finally reaching the heart of the labyrinth. The Minotaur was fast asleep, and though he awoke with a great roar, Theseus quickly defeated the evil monster.

Before he died, the Minotaur bellowed loudly enough to wake the entire palace, so Theseus had to hurry to escape the labyrinth and, with Ariadne's help, free his fellow Athenians. They rushed to their ship and hurriedly put out to sea. Exhilarated by their unexpected freedom, the Athenians forgot to hoist the white sails, and when they entered the harbor at Athens, King Aegeus was so heartbroken at the thought that his son had died that he threw himself into the sea before he could learn the truth.

ABOUT THE AUTHORS

TOM MASON

Besides writing MythQuest and *Malcolm in the Middle* novels, Tom Mason has been the story editor on *Pet Alien*, Nickelodeon's *Brother's Flub*, and several other TV series. He has also written for animation, live action, and even Sony PlayStation games such as Fear Effect: Inferno.

DAN DANKO

Dan Danko has been the story editor on *Pet Alien*, Nickelodeon's *Brother's Flub*, and several other TV series, in addition to writing MythQuest and *Malcolm in the Middle* novels. Dan has written for animation, comic books, infomercials, and even a video game or two.